COURTNEY:
The Puppet Master

Jeremy Jae Jae Davis

Merie Vision Publishing
Merievisionpublishing@gmail.com

Copyright © 2025 by Jeremy "Jae-Jae" Davis
Uptown Classic Productions

ISBN: 978-1-961213-15-9

Library of Congress control number on record

This is a work of fiction. Names, characters, places, and incidents either are the product of the author's imagination or are used fictitiously. Any resemblance to actual persons, living or dead, events, or locales is entirely coincidental.

All rights reserved. No part of this book may be reproduced in any form either by electronic or mechanical means, including information storage and retrieval systems, without written permission from the publisher, except by a reviewer who may quote brief passages in a review.

Formatting, Editing, and Design by
Merie Vision Publishing, LLC

Front Cover by Che'Von

First Print Edition: May 2025

Printed in the United States of America

One

The courthouse was one of the largest infrastructures and historic landmarks located in the contested city of East Orange, New Jersey. Its signature red carpet, along with its antique gold-framed paintings of past judges who once presided there, decorated the hallway walls. Unfortunately, this was a place too familiar to the black community. Her initial goal was to change the narrative in the sentencing guidelines and to put an end to the mass incarceration of African American men and women.

A short, blonde, older-looking, Caucasian priest, dressed in a blue dress suit and red scarf, stood directly in front of her while holding the King James version of the bible. Even though she was a devoted Muslim, she still placed her left hand on top of it, pledging her allegiance. The United States Federal District Court appointed Courtney Latrisha Mendez-Jones as the sixty-eighth Federal District Judge of New Jersey. The entire crowd stood up and applauded. Courtney smiled and waved to her family and friends. Her long-awaited journey to the seat came with hard work and sacrifice.

Courtney graduated at the top of the dean's list from Howard and studied for another four and a half years at Yale. There, she received her master's degree. She went on to work in politics, and eventually landed a job as the Attorney General for the Texas Mayor, Arron Strives. Ultimately, she ran for his position and three years later, she won by a landslide.

The challenges she faced were the political issues, backstabbing, and the antisemitic racism she received from being a black woman in such a high and prominent position. Eventually, it became too overwhelming, and she decided not to run for a second term, unfortunately. Instead, she pursued her love of law, opening her own law firm. Now, she was the lead partner of Courtney, Bryant, Huffman & Associates

After three years in business, her firm was considered to be the best law firm in the state. With thousands of criminal cases dismissed or won on their docket, they had fewer than a hundred convictions. Courtney was considered to be the female Johnny Cockren of her generation. All leading her to this monumental moment of becoming the second woman to ever sit in the chair and the first African American woman to hold the position. She was finally ready to link up with her sister to do what they had planned for decades – shake up the drug underworld and criminal empires.

Before we get into that, let's go back to where this all began...

July 7, 2004, in Norfolk, VA

After discovering their mother had been tragically killed in an assassination, Kandy and Courtney exited their back door and never returned to their home again. After being on the run for thirty-three days from Child Protective Services, she and her eldest sister, Kandy, stayed at a local Motel Six. It was there that they took refuge and tried their best to stay low.

One beautiful Saturday evening, Courtney's sister, Kandy, left her alone for a couple of hours. Not wanting to sit in the confines of the drug-infested motel staring at the walls, she decided to visit the local Military Circle Mall. She thought that would surely kill some time until her sister returned. Just as she was about to exit, a soft knock presented itself at the door.

"It's housekeeping!" a Spanish voice yelled.

Courtney recalled requesting clean linens from the front desk. Unfortunately, as soon as she opened the door, there stood the Spanish housekeeper, but right behind her was Ms. Tracy Williams from social services, along with two Norfolk Police officers.

"Damn!!" Courtney mumbled under her breath.

She couldn't believe she answered the door without looking to see exactly who it was. All she could think of was how distraught Kandy would be when she returned and she was missing. She complied and exited the room with Ms. Williams, but not before noticing her sister slumped down inside the black BMW truck parked in the parking lot. She could spot those gold chains and earrings from far away. Kandy's friend, Keshia, approached Ms. Williams and tried her best to keep her, but Ms. Williams wasn't having any of it. She'd known the Mendez family for quite a while, and she was determined to do what she felt was the right thing to do. She did allow Keshia to leave her phone number with Courtney, while advising her to call her if she knew of Kandy's whereabouts.

"I will," Keshia replied, walking away.

Courtney knew that if anyone knew of Kandy's whereabouts, it would be Keshia. She just prayed her sister would be okay.

Courtney arrived at the social service juvenile center around 3 pm. The environment felt more like a Boys and Girls Club. It was several children eating fried chicken, french fries, and ice cream, while watching music videos. Other kids her age were playing board games like Scrabble and Monopoly. Surprisingly, everyone was nice. She still decided to stay to herself while sitting quietly in the back and observing the scenery. She was able to notice their shortage of staff and how active it was. She knew she could have easily exited through one of the side doors and would have been back Uptown within a matter of minutes. She was very familiar with that section of the city, but for some strange reason, she felt much safer there than back in that drug-infested Motel Six. She was assured by Ms. Williams that she would go to a great home. Six months later, Courtney was adopted by a loving foster family from the Virginia Beach area.

Carlton and Melissa Jones were both retired lawyers. They lived in a two-million-dollar mansion, owned several car dealerships, and three convenience stores. They were the proud parents of two girls, but Courtney was the youngest of the trio by double digits. Their biological daughters, Katrina and Dana, were both headed off to college in the fall to pursue their law degrees. This left Courtney behind, but she was embraced, loved, and inspired by her foster parents to become the best version of herself.

Courtney walked onto the balcony of her thirty-sixth-floor penthouse luxury estate, dressed in her fancy Burberry beige robe. Underneath, she sported a sexy Victoria's Secret red thong and bra, and a pair of six-inch Jimmy Choo limited edition designer heels. She stood a mere 5'7", measuring 34-24-38, and weighed 165 lbs. She stood overlooking the city's beautiful nightlife while sipping her favorite Bella Bolla Moscato white wine and listening to her favorite nineties R&B throwback playlist playing softly in the background. The Jersey night air was crisp, and the well-lit buildings and bright stars illuminated over the Hudson River. She'd had a long and strenuous day serving her justice in the high court today. So, tonight wasn't going to be a Netflix and chill. She decided to invite one of her colleagues over, Steve Savage.

Steve was a Northern Virginian, by way of Philadelphia, who graduated at the top of his class at Yale, turned underworld criminal. He and Courtney met there in the fall of 2008 when he was selling high-grade marijuana and Jello shots from out of his dorm window. Courtney's sex appeal blew him away at first sight. After that, she never paid for another dime bag again.

Steven was considered to be a mad genius because his IQ was amongst the elite. Courtney said he reminded her of Sheldon Cooper from *The Big Bang Theory*, with a little added gangster. It blew Courtney's mind how he studied criminology while indulging in criminal activities. Even within his genius conflicted mind, he harbored a lot of pain.

Back in 2001, his father and his brother were allegedly set up by two undercover DEA agents. They were both wrongly convicted and sentenced to life in prison. So, his belief in the justice system was diluted from his youth. He could care less about the court system. One day, he just wanted to get his family exonerated, which is the motivating drive into who he was each and every day.

At Yale, Steven was the biggest drug dealer, and still, to this present day, it was estimated he brought in millions a week. His massive drug rings ran throughout the East and North boroughs of the city. He was known in the underworld to rule with an iron fist and wouldn't hesitate to kill his opposition or prosecute them in the court of law. His sword was double-sided and a force to be reckoned with. Simply, making him untouchable.

His electoral campaign began months ago, which allowed him to run for Attorney General. Except, for now, he was one of the most corrupt federal prosecutors in the state of New Jersey with Courtney as his sidekick. Somehow, they would always find ways to manipulate the justice system by seeking loopholes and errors in cases or sometimes just looking the other way. They held one thing in common, and that was to fuck over the justice system, while getting to the billion-dollar piece of American pie. This was Courtney's thought process, even while holding one of the most prominent and powerful seats in the United States Courts.

Steve arrived at her home dressed in his usual Tom Ford designer beige double-breasted suit, sporting a solid gold Oyster Rolex watch along with a black Tom Ford alligator briefcase to match his shoes. He didn't waste any time. In fact, as soon as he entered, he began to kiss and caress Courtney.

She quickly turned around and said, "Business before pleasure."

He responded with a slight giggle before reaching into his briefcase and retrieving the federal indictment and arrest warrant for Courtney's sister, Kandy. He had signed off on it and passed her a copy. The second document was a sealed, classified plea bargain. It was for Jah'me to serve no less or more than a year and a day in federal custody.

"Well done," Courtney replied, signing the document while retrieving her copy for her personal files.

By the time she looked up, Steve was standing in the middle of her living room floor naked, snorting lines of pink cocaine, and drinking from the bottle of her favorite wine. She slowly walked over and began caressing Steve's chest. She began rolling up a hundred-dollar bill like a straw and dipped it into his party pack. Then, she snorted three lines. The cocaine and wine combination always made her extra horny. Suddenly, she let her dark and silky hair fall down to the small of her back. She knew that drove him crazy every time. She began teasing him with her tongue, licking his ears, neck, and chest in a sexual and seductive manner, turning them both on, completely. Then, Courtney grabbed Steve's hand and escorted him to her master bedroom suite. On their way there, she intentionally dropped her coat to the floor and exposed her sexy lingerie, six-inch heels, and her undeniable brick-house body.

From there, they decided to role-play. Courtney wanted Steve to act as if he were raping her. She told him whenever she screamed "no" or "stop," that was his signal to get more aggressive and begin choking her while calling her a slutty whore. Strangely, it made her climax even harder, so he was more anxious to oblige.

The next morning, Courtney woke up later than expected. She quickly realized that her alarm clock hadn't gone off. Normally, her security would wake her, but she had left a message instructing her employees to text or leave a message if important. Otherwise, she preferred not to be disturbed.

She rolled over and realized that Steve had left in the middle of the night. She wasn't upset at all because he never stayed over. She knew he was married and had to get back home to his wife, Crystal, and their three kids. So, she got up to see if her cameras recorded their sexcapade. Once again, she had another clear recording of Steve Savage raping her.

She always felt the need to have leverage in any situation. Yes, Steve was good people, but in this life of chess it was all about observation, calculation, manipulation, and always being one step ahead of your opponent. Throughout the years, she learned the game at a high level and had to extort her way through the ranks. Nothing was handed to her. She just mastered the game.

Ryan Reynolds was another one of Courtney's colleagues. The two met when she was the lead partner at her law firm. He was introduced to her through their mutual friend Aaliyah Huffman. Ryan was a federal D.E.A. agent working out of the tri-state area of Philadelphia, New Jersey, and New York, and was also a graduate of Yale. He was the only African American to graduate with his class that year and the first in his family to receive a college degree.

After college, he enrolled in the police academy. After a year of hard training, he graduated as a high-ranking officer. He began to realize that his dreams and aspirations of becoming a dedicated "blue blood" weren't what he had projected when he joined the Massachusetts precinct.

From day one, he realized that his rank meant absolutely nothing when he was assigned to desk duty by his chief. For weeks and hours on end, he sat and typed up hundreds of arrest warrants for judges to sign off on. They even had the audacity to send him on donut and Starbucks runs several times a day for unranked officers and detectives whom he knew for sure weren't qualified to be sitting at his desk. This wasn't college, so why did he feel as if he were being hazed into a sorority? He had worked and studied too hard to be doing inner work for a precinct full of lazy, racist superiors. The perfect career he had projected for himself was starting to look more like a nightmare.

It was a rainy Friday morning around 5 am when he and several undercover agents pursued a narcotics, no-knock arrest warrant. Upon entering, the five suspects were ordered to get on the ground and were handcuffed and detained. Ryan was instructed to get as much information as he could from each suspect to determine if they were illegal aliens or had any warrants.

Upon his investigation, he realized that his captain had searched the entire house and had personally seized a substantial amount of drugs and cash before exiting the residence. Ryan asked his sergeant what was happening.

"Nothing," he replied.

Then, he instructed Ryan to uncuff the white suspects and to book the black ones down at the precinct. He could clearly see that the black suspects were collateral damage, but somebody had to go down with the warrants since the judge had already signed them. That's when he realized the career he had chosen was just as corrupt as the criminals they were arresting.

His captain returned and handed him one kilo of cocaine wrapped in red tape, along with four guns, two assault rifles, and the other two were FN's with green lasers and silencers. He gave them to him to turn into the evidence department. It looked as if the two black men were in trouble because the two white suspects were released out the back door. He knew if they were to go by the book, each suspect would have been booked and arrested, and all the evidence seized would have been weighed, bagged, tagged, and pictures would have been taken. By his professional observation, nothing the agents or detectives ever did during their investigation was legal or according to protocol.

Back at headquarters, he looked at the time and noticed that it was 7 am. His captain was surely going to send him on a Starbucks coffee run. His vehicle was getting serviced, so the captain was going to have to ask someone else. Just as expected, he walked in and instructed Ryan to fetch his coffee. After explaining that his car was getting serviced, the captain reached into his back pocket and tossed him the keys to his police cruiser. The entire drive over, he pondered the whole situation. He couldn't believe how it actually went down. He knew from his teachings at Yale that the suspects' Fourth Amendment rights had been completely violated, and with a good attorney, the case would be thrown out. Systemic racism and corruption were evident in his precinct, and he knew it was only a matter of time before he put in his transfer to either the New Jersey or New York precinct.

Upon leaving Starbucks, just out of curiosity, Ryan decided to pop the trunk of the captain's vehicle. When he did, he discovered a duffel bag with bricks of cocaine wrapped in the same tape as the kilo he was given to turn into the evidence department. He took out his iPhone and took several pictures of the evidence before stepping back and taking another picture of the car and license plate. After their shift was over, Ryan tailed the captain all the way to his residence. He took his phone out again and recorded the captain taking the guns and drugs out of the trunk and entering his house.

A month later, Ryan was asked to report to internal affairs on the third floor of the police precinct. Upon entering, he was instructed to have a seat. Minutes later, a tall, white, redheaded woman walked over and began reading him his rights, after which she asked if he wanted to seek counsel before she continued.

He quickly responded, "No," and asked what he was there for.

The lady walked over with a piece of paper in her hand and began reading him his charges.

"Ryan Reynolds, you are being charged with tampering with evidence and hindering an investigation."

His mouth dropped to the floor. "How is this even possible?" he asked. "I've done my job to the best of my ability with dignity and pride, and this is how the shield repays me?"

She continued, "Upon our investigation, it was estimated to be over twenty kilos of cocaine, and only one was turned in. Mr. Reynolds, this is your signature on this evidence bag with this one kilo of cocaine, correct?"

"Absolutely!" he responded, "But that was all I was given to turn in. There were well over twenty officers on the scene, and I'm the one being charged?"

"Yes," she replied, "unless one of your superiors signs off on it. Otherwise, your career as a cop will be over before it begins," she said before walking away.

Three weeks later, Ryan was cleared of all charges, and his transfer to any precinct he desired was quickly approved.

Two

    Aaliyah Jessica Huffman, also known as Lee-Lee to her friends and family, and Courtney met during their freshman year. The two hadn't been at Yale a week and were already the conversation of the male athletes and jocks on campus. Their sexy features, style, and voluptuous bodies stood out. They couldn't help but attract attention. Plus, the ratio of Black females to white females at Ivy League schools was a staggering nine to one.

    From both their observations, they counted no more than six African Americans on campus in total. In all, it was three women working in the cafeteria, along with Mr. Charles, the male janitor. For Courtney and Lee-Lee, it was their love of law, fashion, and music that connected them as friends, along with the fact that they were both born and raised in the Tidewater area, better known as the Seven Cities.

    Lee-Lee grew up in Great Bridge, a wealthy section of the city. She was the only girl out of four children. Her mother, Lisa, was a retired criminal defense attorney, and her father, Michael Huffman, was a first-round draft pick out of Norfolk State University. He played three years for the New York Knicks, five years for the Oklahoma City Thunder, and overseas in the G-League before ultimately retiring from basketball. She and her three brothers ate, slept, and breathed basketball. They played every day with their father in their exclusive mansion, and their home gym was the size of a regular gymnasium. At twelve years old, Aaliyah could beat two of her talented brothers in a game of twenty-one on any given day.

    One year for Aaliyah's fourteenth birthday, her parents wanted to surprise her by purchasing several Gucci and Prada skirt and jean outfits, along with a leather Gucci purse, a fingernail designer set with over a hundred different polishes and glitters, an iPhone, and several pairs of designer shoes and Ugg boots. The look on her face said it all under her fake smile, and her parents automatically recognized it. As bad as they wanted her to be their sweet little princess, they understood that she was a tomboy and knew exactly what it took to make her happy.

The following weekend, her mother, Lisa, returned all of her girly gifts and drove thirty miles to Dick's Sporting Goods. There, she purchased Aaliyah a brand-new Spalding basketball, three colorful NBA snapback ball caps, and autographed jerseys from Iverson, Kobe Bryant, and Michael Jordan. She bought three pairs of sneakers. She brought the white and red Iversons, the yellow and purple Kobes, and her favorite, the black and red number Jordan 4s. She also brought her a mouthpiece, headband, and armband. After receiving her gifts, Aaliyah told her parents it was the greatest day of her life.

The forecast predicted a seventy-five percent chance of heavy downpours and thunderstorms. Aaliyah decided to get ahead of the storm, so she left her dorm two hours prior to her and Conner's expected dinner date. She arrived at his upscale neighborhood driving Courtney's Acura, blasting the Bose high-quality stereo system. She exited the car wearing a trash bag as a raincoat.

Unbeknownst to her, Conner was entertaining friends and colleagues who taught or worked in the administration departments at Yale, Harvard, and Princeton. He answered the door, surprised to see Aaliyah. The look on his face told her everything she needed to know, especially when he shut the door behind him and joined her in the hallway. That's when she realized he did not want whoever was inside to know she was there to see him.

"You're like two hours early," he said, looking nervous.

"Yeah, I thought I'd beat the weather. Is that a problem?" she asked.

"Kind of...yes and no," he replied.

"So, which is it?" Aaliyah asked, now agitated.

"I have a few friends over…including my ex-fiancé."

"So, what happened to our date night? Had you forgotten all about it?" she asked.

"How could I. That's why the first thing I said was that you were two hours early?"

"Well, are we just going to stand out here in the hallway, or are you going to introduce me to your friends?"

He shook his head no and asked her to come back in two hours, promising he would explain everything to her. Before she could walk away, the door opened, and there stood two drunk gay men.

"Hey!! It's Uber Eats!" the skinny one yelled, clapping his hands.

Aaliyah balled her face up in confusion. Immediately, the men noticed her reaction.

"Well damn! Who peed in your lemonade?" the skinny blonde one asked.

She ignored him, but took the opportunity to glance into Conner's condo. From her observation, it was full of gay men.

"The fuck," she spat before storming off.

Conner followed behind her, pleading his case, but she had seen everything she needed to with her own eyes, clearly.

She turned around and said, "I came over to reveal to you that I'm pregnant with our baby, and this is what I run into?"

"Baby?" he looked at her in shock. "Have you thought about an abortion… the day-after pill… or something?"

"Hell no. I'm not killing my baby," she snapped back.

"And I'm not trying to be your baby's father either," he yelled.

"Well, I guess it sucks to be you. I'll see you in court, Conner Overton III," she said before walking away.

Conner stood at the top of the steps with both hands covering his face. This had to be the worst day of his life. He stood there wondering how he was going to dig himself out of this hole.

Three Months Later

Courtney and Aaliyah were always up to something. After a long conversation, Aaliyah knew exactly what she had to do. Aaliyah entered the Dean of Students' office, now five months pregnant and showing.

"Mr. Overington will see you now," the secretary said, directing her to the side door.

Upon entering, Conner sat at his desk with a disgusted look on his face, but it did not faze her at all. She came to say what she wanted, and if he complied, she would not take him to court.

"I only have fifteen minutes," he said, agitated.

"Good, because it is only going to take me five," she replied.

"Conner, ever since you found out I was pregnant by you, it's like we are enemies."

"I told you I did not want any kids. What can't you understand?"

"I understand that you laid up in the bed with me for months, having unadulterated sex, and now that a child is involved, you are trying your best to exit left."

She pulled out her medical papers and showed him. It clearly read she was twenty weeks along, which was the same time they had begun having unprotected sex.

"I have so much on the line. I could lose my job. You are a freshman, for Christ's sake," he yelled.

She reached into her purse, observed him looking away, and turned off her recorder.

"I can disappear from your life completely, but it is going to cost you."

"How much? A million dollars? Two million?" he asked, pulling out his checkbook.

"Bitch please," she snapped. "I want you to graduate me and two of my best friends at the top of our class and place us on the Dean's List too."

He was silent for a few minutes. Then, he turned around and asked, "Is that all?"

"No," she yelled. "I want five million dollars, cash. That way I can financially support your bastard child."

"Will that be all, Aaliyah?" he asked again.

She stood up and said, "Have my cash ready by next week. After graduation, you will never see me again."

By the time she returned to her dorm, her phone rang. It was Conner.

"You know, I can have you arrested for extortion and bribery," he said aggressively.

She laughed. "I can have you arrested for aggravated rape. Do not play with me, Conner," she said, hitting play on the recorder and letting him hear their earlier conversation.

Seconds later, he hung up.

Later that evening, she received a text message from him saying the money was available and he was working on the graduation arrangements for all three of them.

Courtney laughed, reading the message while watching Aaliyah take off the fake pregnant belly.

"You know what they say in the town – "

"If you can trick 'em, you can beat 'em," they said in unison.

They quickly got dressed and texted Conner the drop-off location. Two hours and fifteen minutes later, they returned with six duffel bags full of crisp, blue-faced hundred-dollar bills. The following Monday, they packed their bags and left Yale, not returning until graduation. Until then, they were about to have the time of their lives. They moved into a luxury condo in Miami and purchased two Mercedes-Benz CL630s. Courtney's was pink and Aaliyah's was burgundy. Life was about to skyrocket for these two bold and brazen freshman criminals.

Courtney was definitely in her bag, and it was full of deceitful tricks. Her black book had enough leverage to turn any blue-collar lawyer, prosecutor, or police officer into a cold-blooded killer. She had mastered her way through the ranks of the underworld and earned her name, the Puppet Master. Under her jurisdiction, she ran the courthouse, the law firms, the police department, and unbelievably, the streets as well. Courtney was a force to be reckoned with and someone you did not want to cross.

On August 12, 2022, she became the CEO of The Firm, a group of higher-learning scholars in powerful positions who the system once tried to destroy or unjustly incarcerate their family or friends. After pledging their allegiance, members of The Firm's main agenda was to take a large chunk of the American trillion-dollar deficit while rewriting the sentencing guidelines throughout the justice system. It had been written in stone and witnessed with her own eyes. This hustle, the ultimate hustle, had secretly been mastered by Caucasians and their mansions for centuries. Now, the blueprint had been exposed to an intelligent Black girl from the ghetto with everything to gain and nothing to lose.

Back at her 36th-floor penthouse, Courtney was relaxing, enjoying her weekend by the fireplace in her robe and fuzzy slippers, eating pizza and ice cream while binge-watching Court TV.

"Oh, hell naw," she screamed at the television. "I would have locked his white ass up the first time he called me a bitch. She better than me," she said while stuffing her mouth.

Her cell phone rang. It was Steve Savage.

He wanted to secure several warrants for a multimillion-dollar drug bust and asked if The Firm could handle all the legal matters, and if possible, he wanted her to assign Ryan Reynolds to the investigation.

"As long as your paperwork is up to par, I do not see any reason why not," she replied, rolling her eyes because she was anxious to get back to her Court TV marathon.

"Yeah, this lick could be the motherload," he said excitedly.

Courtney hung up instantly. She never discussed anything outside of the law over the phone, and Steve knew better. He quickly texted her before leaving to prepare the search warrants. It read,

My bad, Court.

Following Monday Morning

Anthony Brown, an ex-boyfriend Courtney had met in high school, entered her law firm. The two had not seen each other in over a decade. The moment he saw her; he could not believe his eyes.

"Wow, Courtney, you still look the same as you did when we were together...except you have gotten a little thicker in the thigh and hips department. But you are wearing it well," he said, looking her up and down.

"Thank you," she replied, blushing and twirling her braids.

She could not believe her ex-boo-thang had just walked into her office. "You know what they say. If you do not smoke crack, your Black will not crack," Courtney said.

They both burst out laughing, and truth be told, he did not look bad himself. Matter of fact, she still found herself attracted to him.

Anthony had been a certified dope boy from the Uptown section of Norfolk, Virginia. Always sporting the latest fashions, he was charming, kind-hearted, funny, and drove a black S550 Mercedes-Benz. Courtney had been attracted to him at first sight, even though she knew he was a bad boy. They started dating and had a sexual relationship. Courtney would even fly back to Virginia from Yale on the weekends to stay at his luxury condo off Newtown Road. Their relationship lasted over five years until Anthony suddenly did not show up for a date he had promised.

Two weeks later, Courtney found out, through a mutual friend, that Anthony was at Chesapeake General Hospital and welcoming his firstborn son into the world. She called and broke up with him. She was completely heartbroken and swore never to fall for a man like that again, but that was years ago.

Now, living a life of luxury did not always feel so good, not when she had no one to come home to. Many nights, she wished for a man to lay beside her in bed and run on her butt until she fell asleep. However, her dominant thoughts would quickly remind her she was okay alone.

Still, everybody wants love.

Here she was, a decade later, standing in front of the first man she ever loved.

"So, how can I help you?" she asked.

"It is Lamont, my son. He and a few friends broke into an Apple Store down on 136 Market Street. They stole some computers and iPhones, got caught in the act, and the owners pressed charges. I bailed him out this morning and drove straight here, hoping to retain your services. He is a good boy, straight-A student. He has never given me any problems. I do not know what has gotten into him lately."

"Is this the child you were at the hospital for?" Courtney asked.

Anthony smiled. "Yeah. That is him."

Courtney stood up. "I can do you a solid and get all his charges dropped."

"Oh wow, thank you," he said, relieved.

"Consider it my baby shower present," she joked. They both laughed. "But all jokes aside," she said, smiling slyly, "your handsome ass owes me that all-out fun date you promised me twelve years ago and never showed up."

Anthony smirked, remembering vividly. "I was immature and could have handled that a lot better. I sincerely apologize. It would be an honor and a pleasure to make it up to you, beautiful."

Without another word, Courtney picked up her desk phone, made one call, and it was done. She looked over at Anthony and said, "I will see you Friday at 7 p.m. Do not be late."

"Girl, boo! How much money you got for me?"

Courtney asked over the phone, talking to her sister, Kandy.

"Why do you keep charging me, sis?"

"Because your ass can't seem to stay out of trouble. The type of lawyer you need has to be in-house and on standby twenty-four-seven, three-sixty-five! My goodness!" Courtney replied, laughing. "And by the way, I'm not a practicing lawyer any longer, so palms have to be greased. Send me a light two million, and I can have all ten of the females' felonies non-processed due to lack of evidence and no active witnesses. The felony indictment of the male, unfortunately, was captured on video. It's more than likely the prosecution will proceed to get a conviction."

"Okay, I'm wiring the funds to your offshore account," Kandy replied.

"I'm on my banking app now," Courtney reassured her, while staring down at her iPhone.

"You act as if you don't trust me or something," Kandy said, laughing.

"As the late President Reagan once said, trust but verify," Courtney replied.

Kandy was filthy rich, but stingy as hell. She hated paying out of her bag. There were times when Courtney wouldn't have even charged Kandy a dime, but the richer Kandy became, the bigger her problems became. If it wasn't for her, Kandy and her billionaire husband, Jah'me, would have been buried under the prison decades ago.

"By the way, guess who unexpectedly walked into my office this week?"

"Who?" Kandy replied.

"Anthony!"

"Your ex-boyfriend Anthony, from Virginia?"

"Yep, and he still fine as hell," Courtney said.

"But didn't he leave you for that trick, Trina?"

"That was back then. We're talking about now, sis! You know I have issues with dating new men. It's like, if I date my exes, at least I know what I'm getting into. He apologized, and we made plans to go out tomorrow night."

"Ummhmm!" Kandy replied back. "I remember why you love him so much. You miss that baby leg you told me about. I didn't forget, hoe."

They both began laughing their hearts out.

"What is he doing in New Jersey anyways? Did you ever ask him?" Kandy asked.

"I didn't," Courtney replied, "but I'll be sure to pick his brain tomorrow."

Courtney looked down at her banking app. Her Google alert read:

> **You've just received a two-million-dollar Capital One deposit from Jericka Dunkin.**

"I received it! You and all these damn aliases, girl."

"Gotta stay incognito," Kandy replied. "Everyone can't play the big stage like Judge Judy."

"Girl, boo!" Courtney replied.

"I'll keep you posted. Until then, keep your little thugs out of trouble."

"I'll try," Kandy replied, before ending their call.

Before Courtney could even put her phone on the charger, she received another text alert stating she had just received another deposit from Nations Bank for three million five hundred fifty dollars from Kanye Carter. She knew that was another one of Steve Savage's aliases. He must have secured the play from the multimillion-dollar drug bust she signed off on last week and split it three ways with her and Ryan Reynolds.

This was just another day at the office. It was a slow week because Courtney normally averaged five to ten million weekly. She thought about purchasing the new Rolls-Royce truck for her birthday, or she thought that she could finally purchase some land to build her dream home. It just seemed like there was never enough time in a day, but she was determined to make it happen very soon.

Natasha Bryant was a Harvard graduate, law scholar, and CEO of Bryant, Bryant, and Bryant. Her law firm was located in the heart of Brooklyn, New York, and was known for representing some of the biggest names in the entertainment business. She and Courtney crossed paths one evening while attending the Sarah Jakes women's empowerment conference in Houston, Texas. Courtney was exiting her white Rolls-Royce when she spotted a young woman standing beside an all-black Maybach 650, wearing a trench mink coat, a Fear of God black mini skirt and blouse, accessorized with a platinum Cuban choker, matching Rolex watch and bracelet, and sporting a pair of red-bottom, knee-high leather, stiletto boots. Alongside her were two-armed security guards. Courtney knew of Natasha through mutual friends from when she attended Yale. Over the years, she heard from several known associates that Natasha was a powerhouse celebrity lawyer. Courtney began pondering how she could convince Natasha to join her firm. She knew it would legitimize and help it grow to be one of the best law firms in the country. Courtney planned on presenting Natasha with the deal of a lifetime. The question was, would she accept it?

The Firm would generally meet in an undisclosed location of Courtney's choice. She never held meetings at the same establishment and would always wait until the last minute to send out the official meeting location. Today, The Firm was scheduled to meet at an upscale hotel in Maine. The text Courtney sent out read:

Bring your intellectual mindsets, positive energy, and don't forget your bathing suits.

Courtney didn't trust anyone, even though they each took an oath of secrecy. Plus, she knew there was always a weak link in every organization – her brother-in-law Jah'me always told her that. The meeting didn't start until everyone was in the swimming pool. Courtney was the last to walk in, dressed in a sexy white Prada bikini and stiletto heels. Steve Savage and Ryan Reynolds' eyes were glued to her amazing 5'6", 34-24-38, 165 lb. brickhouse frame the minute she dropped her robe and entered the pool. Her security began scanning the pool area for electronic devices. She waited for them to give her the thumbs up before she began talking.

"Good evening! As you all know, the Mexican borders have been heavily secured by the National Guard due to President Trump and his mass deportation tactics. The Sinaloa cartel and border patrol can't move our product. We're now at a standstill, so in order to meet our billion-dollar quota, we have to raise the prices."

"Not if we cut the product ourselves," Steve replied. "We're buying it at wholesale rates anyway and have never cut or stepped on it before distribution. If, unfortunately, we're forced to have to go through this drought period, instead of raising the prices, I strongly suggest we cut the product. That way, we keep our base clientele."

"But the product won't be as pure," Courtney said, looking confused.

"It's a drought, boss lady! I can't imagine any product being pure from this point on until this drought is over. Most distributors would rather be with, than without," he replied.

"Does everyone agree with Steve?" Courtney asked. They each shook their heads yes. "Then we will set up shop and have the product cut and ready for distribution within the Tri-State immediately."

"I have a partner down at the DEA's office who's supposed to be getting me a few shipments that were recently seized from the Gulf of Mexico and scheduled to be destroyed. I'm going to see if we can pull a few strings to get a container or two sent to our customs loading dock. If that doesn't work out in our favor, I have a few trump cards in the deck. Either way, we're going to eat off of this drought," Courtney said.

"The Firm!" Courtney said sternly with authority.

She made sure she made eye contact with each individual in the pool. "Is a sworn secret society, a well-educated and powerful brother and sisterhood who have all discovered and cracked open the blueprint that the Masons and the founding fathers implemented on our society. By capitalizing and cornering the market on their make, names, images, and joint business ventures. Each one of you has sworn to harbor that secret until death and will be held accountable not only to know your position in the Firm, but to perfect it. Our bail bondsman venture brought in some astronomical numbers this quarter after signing the arrest warrants for an all-out sweep. I personally set most of their bails at five hundred thousand to a million dollars. We confiscated over half a ton of cocaine and put it right back on the streets while providing the street-level dealers with the best defense attorneys in the city."

She looked at each of them again. "Each of you is aware that The Firm has a twenty-five percent shareholder account with the New Jersey Nets and another thirty percent with the New York Jets. We also have a forty percent shareholder account with the WNBA's new Unrivaled. I believe once we close the fifty percent stake on this WNBA team, it's billionaire status for us all before age fifty."

Everyone listened on with a smirk on their faces. "It's estimated that we've brought in close to five hundred million in the last quarter. Your smart investments paid off. Let's continue to invest and allow our money to make money for us. Financial freedom and generational wealth are the end goals."

Courtney looked back at her CFO, Kimberly, giving her the okay to wire transfer their funds.

"In a few minutes, your funds should be hitting your accounts." She thanked them all for attending before adjourning her meeting.

Courtney exited the pool. Immediately, you noticed her wet, silky, dark hair along with her voluptuous body dripping water. You couldn't help but notice the detailed Scorpio covering her entire back and ass. She didn't even care to cover up. She just walked away, dripping wet with both her security guards at her side. This was the only way she ever held her personal meetings. The Firm never discussed anything outside of the law over the phone.

Ryan Reynolds shook his head, watching Courtney walk away.

"UmmmHmmm, lawdy! I sure would like to see what that stuff is hitting for," Ryan said, shaking his head.

Steve Savage didn't even respond. Normally, men would tell one another if they had sex with a beautiful woman, but he knew that keeping his mouth shut was the very reason he often got to tap it. Not wanting to mess that up, he decided to keep his mouth shut.

⬩

Courtney decided to reintroduce herself. She knew if she were going to come at Natasha Bryant with a business proposal, it was going to have to be one that was box office. Because Natasha was already a successful, rich, and powerful lawyer, she knew she had to come correct.

"I remember you," Natasha said. "We met through my girl Aaliyah Huffman at Yale."

"Of course," Courtney replied, not actually remembering, but since it was through Aaliyah, it was an added bonus.

"Wow! She works at my law firm in New Jersey. We're expanding our services and will soon be opening new offices in Miami and on the West Coast. My end goal is to have law offices up and down the East and West Coast," Courtney said.

"Those are some very powerful goals," Natasha said.

"I'm a very powerful woman," Courtney added.

"And that you are," Natasha concurred. "I aspire to be like you one day holding a federal seat. Congratulations, Judge."

"Thank you, but what I need is someone like yourself to partner with while growing and expanding my law firm. As you know, I'm currently a full-time judge, but I need someone with your intellectual law intelligence to run my company," Courtney said.

"Wouldn't that be a conflict of interest? Me working at your law firm while holding a federal trial in your courtroom?"

"Sure is. That's why you will be running the company. My last name is actually Jones, by the way, not Courtney. So, the firm's name shouldn't hinder us."

Natasha looked up at the night sky before talking. "It's just, I've put so much hard work into building my own legacy that I never imagined working for anyone ever again."

"I'll give you a fifty-million-dollar signing bonus, a luxury thirty-sixth-floor penthouse with a security detail, and a luxury company vehicle of your choice. I will also pay you a 175k monthly salary."

Natasha looked at Courtney and knew she was serious. "I can most definitely jump for that offer," she said, smiling from ear to ear.

"Then welcome to Courtney, Bryant, Huffman and Associates."

The two women exchanged numbers and went their separate ways with plans to meet up.

Three

Anthony Brown was indeed Courtney's first love. In fact, she was his first love as well. However, their relationship came to a sudden halt after his discovery of a newborn son. Anthony felt that it wasn't just his responsibility, but it was his obligation to be there for his son. He had grown up an orphan, without siblings or the love and guidance of his parents. There was no way he could allow his own blood to experience what he had gone through, mentally, emotionally, and spiritually, growing up without a father to teach him what a real man was. Most of all he had to teach him how to survive as a Black man in a white man's world.

The story he had been told was that his mother, Monica, and his father, Anthony Sr., had died on a snowy Christmas Eve around midnight in a head-on collision with a drunk driver. Anthony Jr. had been born just a few days before his mother was medically cleared and discharged from The Chesapeake General Hospital. Allegedly, they were headed home for his first Christmas when their vehicle was discovered, crushed like a soda can on I-664. Firefighters and EMS rushed to the scene, only to witness the horrific aftermath. EMS stated that they kept hearing faint cries echo from the wreckage after pronouncing the two adults dead on arrival. The jaws of life were used, and in the backseat of the car, they discovered a newborn baby boy, unscathed, sitting in his car seat.

Over the years, Anthony was raised in several foster homes and group homes. Growing up as a troubled youth, life was always rough. For a twelve-year-old in a drug-infested, impoverished community, he looked at the older drug dealers and aspired to have more than they could ever imagine. He knew that once he received a package, he would blow up because he had nothing to lose and so much to gain. That day came sooner than expected.

It was a Saturday evening, around six, when he and several of his friends were playing a pickup game of basketball. It was getting dark, and it seemed like every dope boy in the project had come out to play ball or show off their expensive rides and flashy gear. The music played loudly, and people danced while grilling hot dogs and hamburgers. Suddenly, four armed men walked over and began shooting. It was a direct hit, as they didn't shoot at anyone except that particular group of drug dealers sitting under a tree. People screamed and scattered at the sound of the gunshots. They all ran in different directions. Anthony stood frozen on the basketball court, unable to move, and watching in horror as the four men walked up, executing the wounded.

He counted several dead victims. He recognized the tall, light-skinned Spanish man with golds in his mouth the moment he lifted his mask. They called him Slim, a well-known gangster and pimp in the community. Anthony vividly recalled hearing Slim say to one of his henchmen, "Spare the youngin'."

"But he seen our faces," one of the shooters replied.

"I be seeing this little soldier out here all the time," Slim responded. "He's one of the real ones. I can always spot 'em." Slim turned to Anthony. "He didn't see anything, right?"

Anthony shook his head. "No."

Slim paused for a moment before speaking again. "Do me a solid, lil' youngin'. Pick up all the gun shells you see on the ground and throw them in the sewage drainage over there. Hurry up, before the police get here." Slim reached into his pocket, handed him a crisp, blue-faced hundred-dollar bill, and said, "This is for your time and most of all, your loyalty. I'll see you around."

Anthony collected every shell. In the process, he ran each of the dealers' pockets. In total, he walked away with nine hundred dollars in cash, two ounces of marijuana, and three ounces of crack cocaine. It was a newfound treasure. He understood that failure wasn't an option and he had to make it count.

Two Years Later...

At age thirteen, Anthony started going by "Ant" and was recognized as one of the up-and-coming dope boys Uptown. He lived at the local, run-down Economy Lodge, where he and two of his runners sold drugs out of rooms 312, 317, and 319. Anthony had become a product of his environment. He was cold-hearted and ruthless when it came to his drugs and money. Over time, hustling and leadership had become second nature. However, for some strange reason, he could never get past the ten-thousand-dollar hump. After paying for his weekly hotel rooms, his runners, food, and clothes, he always seemed to be stuck at that same amount and was unable to get ahead.

One Saturday night, as he went to get ice from the machine, he ran into a gorgeous older woman with slanted eyes standing in front of the snack machine. Just then, a familiar figure walked out of a room beside them, flanked by two women. Anthony knew that face and that cocky aura anywhere.

"Aye, Slim!" he called out, stopping the man in his tracks.

Slim squinted at him for a moment. "Do we know each other?"

"It's me, lil' youngin'!" Anthony said with a wide grin.

Slim tilted his Gucci sunglasses down to the edge of his nose. Recognizing him he replied, "Youngin', I been waiting on you," showing a light smile and flashing his gold teeth.

The 36th-floor penthouse was an elegant two-story marvel in the heart of the business district. The 42,000-square-foot estate took Natasha's breath away the moment she stepped inside. The space was immaculately designed, featuring a stunning indoor waterfall and cream-and-gold marble floors. The open floor plan oozed style and grace, and the floating spiral glass stairs led to a secured master bedroom with a balcony that offered sweeping views of the Hudson River, the Tri-State area, and the Statue of Liberty.

The garage housed five luxury vehicles, and the valet service offered additional parking for guests. There was also a law library and computer room. This was any lawyer's dream.

As she stood on the balcony, taking in the view, Natasha felt like she had finally made it to the top. The business district below looked like a line of small ants, and she felt like their new queen. Her daydream was interrupted when she heard a pair of heels approaching.

"Greetings, Natasha!" Courtney walked up and embraced her, accompanied by her Chief Financial Officer, Kimberly. "How do you like the penthouse?" Courtney asked.

"Oh, my goodness, where do I even start?" Natasha said, her smile lighting up her face. "I didn't know you could find something this chic and elegant in New Jersey."

"It has more of an LA vibe when you enter," Courtney said.

"I love it!" Natasha replied, plopping down on the plush white sectional.

"Glad you like it. Now, let's get you paid. Do you have any questions first?"

"Maybe one or two," Natasha replied with a sly smile.

"Okay, the floor is yours." Courtney replied as she spread her arms wide open.

"Now, I know this is a business, but how much of this signing bonus is actually guaranteed?" Natasha asked.

"Fifty million," Courtney answered confidently.

"Wow!" Natasha exclaimed. "And my salary of a hundred and seventy-five thousand a month remains the same no matter how much the firm grosses?"

"Period," Courtney confirmed.

"And will I ever receive the deed to this penthouse?"

Courtney pointed to Kimberly, who was opening a briefcase with the contract for the law firm, the signing bonus, the deed to the penthouse, and the title to Natasha's brand-new, two-hundred-thousand-dollar champagne-colored Rolls-Royce Wraith. It still had the sticker on the window.

Natasha, being the top scholar she was, knew how to assess contracts very well. She excused herself and took the next twenty-five minutes to read over each one of them. Courtney wasn't offended at all. As a matter of fact, she loved it. This was the type of person she wanted around her at all times. Someone who took the business just as seriously and professionally as she did. From the looks of it, Natasha was that person.

Natasha looked up and said, "The only thing missing in the contract is me being CEO of Courtney, Bryant, and Huffman."

Courtney looked at her and said, "Haven't I given you enough? I've financially secured you for a lifetime, and you haven't earned a single dime yet. I will never sign over my business. You have my word that you will be the lead partner and face of the firm. Is that good enough?"

Natasha looked around at the penthouse, back at Courtney, and began signing the contracts. Courtney looked at Kimberly and gave her the thumbs up to proceed with the wire transfer. Two minutes later, Natasha received a text from her Capital One bank stating that fifty million dollars had been deposited into her business account.

"Oh, my gawd. I have never seen this many zeros in my account."

"This is only the beginning," Courtney assured her.

Courtney popped the cork from the bottle of Ace of Spades, passed Natasha and Kimberly a wine glass, and made a toast to success, longevity, billions of dollars, and Courtney, Bryant, Huffman, and Associates.

Kimberly Martin was Courtney's Chief Financial Officer. She and Courtney met her senior year at Yale. They were both attending the same business finance class. Kimberly was a math genius. She was known around campus as the human calculator. For a side hustle, she did everyone's federal and state income taxes each year, including the students and even some of the top Yale administrative workers.

Her major was computer technology and cybersecurity. She graduated with honors and landed her dream job at NASA in Houston, Texas. It was there that she met Brian Adams. He was her supervisor. Kimberly was highly attracted to him, but he was married and had been up front telling her that he just wanted to have sex with no strings attached.

After having a couple of hot flings at the office, their sexual relationship simmered down, and Brian began ignoring her calls. Suddenly, she succumbed to scrutiny and daily sexual harassment. It was revealed to her from a coworker that Brian had been taping their sexual encounters and was seen showing them to the entire office.

Because of this, she was often lied on, men began saying she was easy, and they started saying they had slept with her. She found herself being groped on by men while walking and disrespectfully being called a slutty black whore.

Eventually, she had a mental breakdown, she quit her job, and filed a multimillion-dollar lawsuit against several coworkers and NASA. That's when she decided to hire Natasha to represent her. After several long months of court procedures, NASA and three of her coworkers settled out of court for a substantial amount of money.

Kimberly still wanted to live out her dreams and aspirations of becoming a scientist. So, she applied for work at different NASA establishments. As soon as they realized who she was, they would automatically tell her to reapply whenever they posted an opening on their website. After several failed attempts, she realized that her dreams of becoming a scientist were over. Her lawsuit against NASA had blackballed her from ever working for any of their establishments or government contractors again.

One year later, Kimberly bumped back into Natasha at the *Something in the Water* annual festival held in Virginia Beach, Virginia. The two of them embraced, and Kimberly told

Courtney her story. The following Monday, Courtney called and surprised her with a job offer she just couldn't refuse.

Anthony arrived at Courtney's luxury ranch estate located in the hills of Hartford, Connecticut. It was his first time ever visiting the state, as well as Courtney's extravagant home. He couldn't believe how enormous it actually was. The estate sat deep back in a cul-de-sac of a secluded gated community. If he hadn't used his GPS, he would have driven right past it. Upon arrival, Anthony took notice of the foreign fleet of luxury vehicles parked along the driveway. As soon as he approached the estate, he was greeted right away by her six-foot-seven, 250-pound butler, Mr. Dixon.

Mr. Dixon was an older gentleman in his early to mid-sixties. He had a serious demeanor and didn't smile much. Anthony could tell by his aura and his physical appearance that he was either a retired police officer or an ex-military special forces. He also noticed the armed security guards walking back and forth doing perimeter checks along the property. For his first impression, he was quite impressed, but not surprised.

"Evening, sir," he said with a deep British accent. "The Misses awaits your arrival."

He entered the estate following Mr. Dixon. Anthony had always known that Courtney was wealthy, but damn, had she hit the jackpot and not told a soul? He looked around in awe. *This estate has to be around seventy-five thousand square feet or more,* he thought to himself. He knew for sure that his mansion back in Virginia could fit inside of this mega mansion twice.

"*Courtney is doing more than just serving justice,*" he said, looking at the high Baltic ceilings. He was definitely going to find out, though.

He was asked to have a seat inside the master quarters. Upon entering, the soft scent of lavender and peach, combined with the cedarwood burning in the fireplace, smelled amazing. The soothing sounds of Regina Belle played throughout the surround sound system. Mr. Dixon walked over and offered him a drink. He kindly accepted while looking around. He couldn't help but notice the Picassos hanging above her mantle, along with the Andy Warhols. He recalled being present at the London auction house when one of Warhol's paintings went for twenty-five million, and it was way smaller than the one in front of him. He also took notice of the pictures of the Seven Cities, where they were both from. It had been a while since he'd been back home, so the photos had him punch drunk.

Courtney had framed images of the Norfolk Scope Arena, the Harbor Park Baseball Stadium, the iconic Waterside, and Nauticus Water and Science Museum. She also had several pictures of her cheerleading squad standing in front of Booker T. Washington High School...where they first met and fell in love.

"Looks like somebody's stuck back on memory lane," a light, sexy voice said from behind.

He turned around, and there she was, standing in a sweatsuit and a pair of Jordans, with her hair braided. "Heey! Boo," he said. "You look..." He paused, looking her up and down.

"I know you're used to seeing me in high heels and a skirt," she said, walking over to hug him, "but I just wanted to relax and have a great time with you tonight."

Anthony wasn't tripping. Courtney looked good in anything she wore. Plus, that ass was busting out of them sweats. He couldn't believe how thick and pretty she actually was. She reminded him of Janet Jackson back in her *Poetic Justice* days.

"You smell amazing," he complimented her. "Is it Prada Candy?"

She smiled and replied, "Yes. You smell great as well. Let me guess," she said, sniffing his neck. "Ummm, one of my favorites... is it Versace Blue Jeans?"

"Okay!!" Anthony said, laughing. "I just feel overdressed now."

"No worries," she replied. "We can stop and get you a sweatsuit too!"

He burst out laughing. "We're definitely not dressing alike. I know what I'm wearing," he said, still laughing.

"What are you wearing?" she asked in her sexy voice before she began kissing all over him.

He looked down at her and said, "Nothing."

"That's exactly what I was thinking too," she replied, watching him undress. "I know that's right," she added. "But wait, let's take this show to my bedroom."

The elevator to her room happened to be directly to their right. Courtney entered and pressed her handprint onto the computer board. Suddenly, the elevator doors closed, and they began to move up. Anthony continued to kiss and caress her body the entire time. As soon as the door opened, they were both nearly naked as she guided him to her California King-size bed. Then, the two of them had hot, unadulterated sex for the remainder of the evening.

Anthony woke up three hours later and noticed Courtney wasn't in bed. Just when he was about to get dressed, she walked back in, drinking a cup of tea.

"How did you rest?" she asked.

"Good. Real good. You?"

"I slept for an hour, but you know I don't sleep much."

"I must not have done my job," Anthony said.

"Oh yes, you did," she said, sipping her tea.

"So, you live in this extravagant estate all alone?" he asked.

"No. My butler, security, and my assistant, Kimberly, all live here with me. It's a sight for sore eyes, and it's humongous."

"Why did you choose to move into an estate of this magnitude?"

"Why not?" she replied.

Anthony laughed. "I can dig it, baby," he said, kissing her on the neck.

"You're asking me a hundred questions. How about I start asking some?"

"Okay, shoot 'em at me. I know you have some," he replied.

"So, what brought you to New Jersey, and how did you find me?"

"My son, AJ. He's been staying out in East Orange with his mother for the summer. I've basically been raising him myself. He's my heart, and I only want to see him grow into a respectable and honorable man. Somehow, he and three of his friends from the neighborhood decided to steal iPhones. I'm guessing he's easily influenced, because the last time I checked, he had over a hundred thousand in his savings account. Thanks to you, he's home with his mother on punishment instead of in a detention center." He smiled.

"I was looking for an attorney for AJ when Michelle, my assistant, said she heard of the law firm of Courtney, Bryant, Huffman and Associates…being the best on the East Coast. She googled the website, and that's when I discovered your beautiful face standing beside the other two women. That's when I knew I had to visit your establishment, with hopes of getting you or someone from your law firm to represent my son in court."

"Ummmhmm," Courtney replied.

Being a judge, she was good at reading people. She could tell he was being upfront and sincere.

"So, what's your story? Are you still in the streets?" she asked.

"I'm always going to be tied to the streets. You know I've been a hustler since I stepped off the porch. But on the entrepreneurial side of things, I've been in the real estate and transportation business for over a decade."

"Do tell," she said, sipping her tea.

"I have several box trucks and six Sprinter vans on the highways and byways, 24/7, 365. They move packages locally and statewide. I also have partners at the Navy Federal Bank who call me weeks before they post their foreclosures. So, I get to bid on the best houses and estates before they're even put out to the public. As of today, I've closed on between twenty-five and thirty homes. Fifteen of them were mansions, and fifteen were modern-sized middle-class homes. I can honestly say I brought in roughly around thirty million in 2024."

"That's not bad at all, Anthony. How much did you make in the underworld?" Courtney asked, poking her lip out like she already knew.

Anthony was quiet for a second before responding. He wasn't crazy. He knew who he was dealing with. There was no need to hold back any information, because she could easily find out with the snap of her finger. Maybe, she'd already done her homework and wanted to see if he would lie.

He replied that he did more than fifty million in sales between the states and overseas. He was currently living in New Jersey, pushing most of his product throughout the Tri-State area.

"Thank you for being open and honest with sharing your personal information with me," she said.

"So, tell me something," Anthony said.

"Anything," she replied.

"How can you afford to live a life so lavish? I know this estate is fifty to a hundred million easy."

She looked him straight in the face and said, "You know I'm president of my own law firm and I'm also a sitting United States federal judge."

"So, you holding back on me, bae? Anthony asked.

"I know there's more to your story. You down with the Masons or something? I heard all women judges are Northern Stars."

Courtney burst out laughing while shaking her head.

"I don't believe you," he replied. "You a Northern Star?" he asked again.

Courtney's entire demeanor shifted. He was starting to get in over his head. She suddenly stood up and said, "Those who know, don't tell. And those who tell, don't know. I heard that's how it's been, and always will be," she replied with a serious look.

Courtney woke up the next morning and realized she'd missed an important call from her partner, James Cook, over at the DEA office. If he was calling, it meant the containers were available. She couldn't have been more excited. Sure, she always had her sister Kandy in the cut, but Kandy didn't have the time or patience for large-scale moves. She was too busy counting pennies. With James, things were smoother. Most of the time, it was a flat rate no matter how much cocaine or heroin was loaded in the container. His price never changed.

Courtney walked into her grand room where Kimberly sat, waiting with her laptop open. She immediately returned the call.

"Hello," James answered.

"Greetings! It's a beautiful day. Just returning your call," Courtney said.

"Yes, I called earlier to let you know your Boston Celtics are playing at the Garden tonight. Just wondering if you'll be attending."

"How are the ticket prices?" she asked playfully.

"They're worth the rate for where we'll be sitting. Can't beat it...times five."

"Okay, I'll have my assistant book my flight tonight."

Their actual conversation was coded, but clear between the lines:

"Hello," he answered.

"Can you talk?" she asked.

"Yes," he replied.

"Your container will be at the loading dock in Boston. Will you be attending tonight?"

"Are the numbers still the same?" she asked.

"Yes. Product is pure China white and worth every dollar. You can cut it five times."

"Okay. I'll have someone on the next flight out."

Back at the law firm, Natasha and Aaliyah were hard at work. Natasha hadn't had time to decorate her new office, so she hired an interior designer to do it within 24 hours. She was deep into high-profile celebrity cases she'd taken on before joining Courtney, Aaliyah, Huffman & Associates. Her office stayed packed with hip-hop celebrities and pro athletes. Her recent wins with ASAP Rock and Mitch Mill brought her serious attention. Her current roster included Lucci and Shiesty, and even Lil Durk, who was fighting a conspiracy to commit murder and a RICO charge. She turned down a case from the notorious Diddy Do It. Sometimes the headache just wasn't worth the money.

Courtney pulled up to the warehouse in her black Rolls-Royce truck. Ryan and Steve Savage were already waiting. They both entered her vehicle.

Ryan spoke first. "Courtney, we received the container last night. It arrived at the Boston pier, not the usual customs dock. It's estimated to be a metric ton. It's worth over five hundred million in street value."

"Estimated?" Courtney asked, surprised.

"Pretty much. We won't know the exact amount until it's broken down and distributed. But we *do* know we can triple our fifty-million-dollar investment," Steve Savage said.

"Then let's get to work," Courtney replied. "Move the product. Get it on the streets ASAP. Put the rest of The Firm on standby. Let them know, it's game time."

Courtney finally made it back to her Connecticut estate after a long ten-hour day serving justice. Her court docket had been packed with immigration cases. Ever since the new president took office, her courtroom had seen a 75% rise in deportations, which cut deep into her usual 85% drug caseload.

She kicked off her red-bottom stilettos and sat in front of the fireplace, sipping her white wine, reflecting on her day, and on Anthony.

The pros of introducing him to The Firm went beyond their romantic chemistry. She knew him well...his habits, his past, every debt he'd ever owed. Hell, she even remembered his overdue beeper bill from 1998. More than that, he was solid. He hadn't been incarcerated since he was a juvenile. His credit score was 775. His personal finances... well over a hundred million hidden in multiple Swiss bank accounts throughout the South Pacific and Gulf regions.

She didn't expect him to reveal the full extent of his wealth, but she knew he was holding back. She suspected he had another fifty million he didn't mention.

"Men..." she muttered, scrolling through her iPhone.

Kimberly had already sent a report that his trucking and real estate businesses checked out. *Legit.* He'd been honest from the beginning about his dealings in the underworld. Was he the missing piece?

Right now, Steve Savage was her only street-level advisor. While reliable, she wanted a second opinion from someone who understood the streets, but wasn't *in* the streets. She could use Anthony's empty homes as stash houses. His trucking company could handle local and statewide deliveries. In exchange, he'd get a 5% stake in her empire.

He'd nailed it!

She *was* holding back. She *was* a Northern Star Mason, but she'd die before admitting it to him. The real question? *What did Anthony value most? What did he love so much he couldn't bear to lose?* Once she figured that out, maybe... just maybe... she'd consider letting him pledge his allegiance to The Firm.

Courtney's phone rang around 12:03 a.m. When you're a sitting judge, you have DEA and ATF agents calling you to sign no-knock drug warrants and indictments. She had her glasses and robe ready, but to her surprise, it wasn't an agent...it was Steve Savage.

"Happy birthday, gorgeous!"

"Oh, thank you, Steve. You're the first to tell me," she said, rolling her eyes.

"I wanted to know if I could stop by and give you some of this birthday ding-a-ling."

She burst out laughing. "No fool!"

"Why not?" he asked, surprised.

She had been allowing him to slide by and knock her boots almost every two weeks, and it had been almost a month and a half.

"I'm back with my ex-boyfriend, and he's been blowing my back out every day since we met back up. I'm still in my recovery stage right now. I'm sorry for my bluntness, but it's the truth."

"Damn!! It's like that, Courtney?"

"It's only sex. I'm not your girl, Steve. You have a wife named Crystal and three kids at home. Stop acting crazy. I gave you the real. It was good while it lasted, but right now, the only thing making me cum is some damn money! By the way, I just put an MT on the streets, and here you are talking pillow talk. I think you should tighten up and get to the bag, my boy. Until then, for future references, let's keep this professional."

Steve Savage knew Courtney was referring to the Metric Ton of cocaine she had recently purchased and distributed onto the streets, but he could care less at the moment. He wanted to know just who this ex-boyfriend was.

The following morning, Courtney was back at the law office of Courtney, Bryant, Huffman and associates and having a private meeting with Aaliyah. She wanted to know any updates on Natasha or Anthony.

"Well... with Anthony...I've spotted a red flag!" Aaliyah said. "It's like this. For a street nucca, his rap sheet is way too clean. I checked all the police files and police academies on the East Coast, and there's no record of him. So, we can scratch out him being a cop. Are you for sure his name was Anthony Brown when you two were together back in the day?"

"One hundred percent," Courtney replied.

"He does have a son by the name of Anthony Brown Jr. His mother, Angela Brown, lives in Suffolk, VA. He also has a residence in Suffolk, and he recently purchased an apartment in New Jersey. Other than that, Anthony checks every box, but that's the red flag. o one ever checks all the above boxes. I think it's another chapter to him that hasn't been revealed, yet."

39

"And what's been going on with sister girl?" Courtney asked, referring to Natasha.

"My goodness!! You must have crowned her queen of the Wakanda law firm because she been directing orders since she walked in the door. Out of love and respect for you, I bit my tongue several times. I had to remind her that I'm not a paralegal. My name is on the building too trick!"

"You stupid!" Courtney said laughing.

"Other than that, she's professional and a workaholic. She brings a lot of experience and knowledge to our firm. She also has a large celebrity client base."

"Yeah, I meant to tell you that," Courtney replied. "Is she nosey? Has she been asking questions about our client base and income?" Courtney asked.

"Nope! Not at all! She's happy, content, and brags and boast all day about what she's buying next. You must have really dropped the bag."

"I did, but only because I know she is worth every dollar. Stay positive, productive and keep me posted on any new updates."

"I will," Aaliyah replied. "Oh, and happy birthday, sis. I didn't forget!" She said with a smile.

"Thank you." Courtney said before exiting.

Courtney had a scheduled lunch date with Anthony. She thought about discussing real estate and home renovations with him. Back in college, she was interested in becoming a realtor and she had become interested in purchasing a few acres down in South Florida, Los Angeles, or in the Hollywood Hills. She also wanted to purchase a vacation getaway home. She figured she could Airbnb any of them during the summer or winter whenever she didn't stay there.

She was deep in her thoughts when Anthony finally pulled up ten minutes late. He pulled in beside her Rolls-Royce, in his white Mercedes-Benz. Then, he exited his vehicle and entered hers.

"Good evening, and Happy birthday," he said as he kissed her.

"Thank you, but you're late!" she said, rolling her eyes.

"So what? I'm not one of your business partners. I'm your man." he replied in a cocky tone, while leaning over to kiss her sexy lips again.

It was rare that someone talked to her that way. The men she dated were usually timid around her. Indeed, she was and had always been a Boss and alpha female, but she knew she could submit to a man of his caliber. In all, it just felt refreshing to be told to shut up and what to do sometimes.

Every time she was around Anthony, she blushed and folded in his arms like a wet paper napkin. It was amazing how she still harbored those same feelings after almost two decades. As soon as Anthony finished scrolling through his iPhone, he asked, "What would you like to eat?"

"Surprise me!" she replied.

Without saying another word, he leaned forward and instructed her driver, Mitchell, to head over to Manhattan's famous, Plaza Hotel. As soon as they arrived, the valet service accepted their keys. Courtney stepped out and looked stunning. Her freshly done braids looked like new money hanging from under her stylish black hat. She wore a black Fendi peacoat, a red and black Fendi blouse, a black Christian Dior dress, and a pair of red knee-high boots. Her accessories were a platinum Cuban link choker, a set of diamond hoop earrings, a platinum oyster Rolex watch, and a pair of Dior designer shades. She couldn't hide her wealth if she tried. Anthony was dressed casually in an all-white Tom Ford button-up, fitted pants, a pair of polo boat shoes, a plain Jane Rolex, and a diamond bracelet and pinky ring. He made sure to put on her favorite Cologne, Versace Blue Jeans.

The Plaza Hotel was unique. It catered to some of New York's wealthiest clients and celebrities. Its menu had some of the finest cuisines from master chefs from all over the globe.

"This food is amazing! So, how many women have you brought here?" Courtney asked, looking around

"This is actually my first time here smart ass! A good friend of mine asked me to check it out the next time I'm in town with a beautiful woman. I figured I would make reservations. But this amazing food is far from the surprise I have for you," he said.

"Okay!!" she replied.

Anthony stood up, took her by the hand, and walked towards the elevator. As soon as they stepped in, she began thinking that he must have rented an exclusive penthouse and was taking her up for a typical romantic nightcap with R&B music, candles, and wine by the fireplace. Soon, she realized that things weren't playing out the way it had in her head. In fact, they exited onto the roof of the Plaza Hotel, and the weather couldn't have been more perfect. Once there, she spotted a helicopter parked on a massive helipad.

"Come on, baby!" Anthony said while holding her hand.

The pilot noticed them walking towards the helicopter and he quickly exited to open the door. Courtney was in awe already. Once in, they put on their headset, strapped their seatbelts, and within the next two minutes, they were up in the air, flying away into the beautiful New York City nightlife.

"It's beautiful up here!" Courtney said as she looked at the millions of glowing buildings, bridges, and cars in traffic as they flew over the Brooklyn Bridge.

Jay-Z and Alicia Keys' hit song "Empire State of Mind" played through their headphones as the two of them sang along, sipping glasses of Ace of Spades champagne.

"Happy Birthday, baby!" he passed her a rare blue rose and made a toast to lasting love.

"You are too much!" She said, looking over at him and pointing at the Statue of Liberty.

The helicopter circled the Statue of Liberty twice and flew over the iconic Yankee Stadium once before heading back to Manhattan. Courtney hadn't had an experience on a date like this ever. She had to say she was quite impressed, drunk, and ready to undress.

The Robert H. Holman Federal Court Building was proceeding with the expected drug cases today. It had been several weeks, and she had signed one hundred drug indictments and no-knock warrants. Judge Jones stepped up to the podium and opened her case load. From the looks of things, the drug supply she put out on the streets was selling. Today's docket held thirty possession with intent to distribute cases, for which she granted each a bond for fifty thousand dollars. She also held forty drug trafficking cases and twenty drug and weapons cases. In those cases, she also granted bonds of a million dollars. She also suggested they seek the court-appointed counsel or the services of Ms. Bryant and the bondsman in the back.

Around the time she recessed, she was given an accurate update that 60% of offenders had bailed out and had also sought representation by Ms. Bryant and Ms. Huffman. *Not bad at all*, she thought to herself as she looked over the numbers in her chambers. Then, she dialed Ryan Reynolds number.

"Hello!"

"Ryan, this is Judge Jones."

"Good evening, Judge."

"I called to get a report on the evidence discovered and confiscated from my caseload today."

"From my knowledge, it's at least 55% in drugs reported and 25% in weapons."

"Okay, thank you for your service," she said before ending the call.

From her assessment, it was a great day. Now, all they needed to do was to get her drugs, dealers, and guns back on the streets immediately. However, unbeknownst to her, she was being followed and recorded on video by one of her very own, Steve Savage. He followed her and Anthony to the Plaza Hotel. Then, he sat in the parking garage for more than twenty hours waiting for her Rolls-Royce truck to move. He still had a sour taste in his mouth from their last conversation, and he had to find out who this mystery man was that had been taking his place in the bedroom. Not only was he keeping her away from him, but she was also slacking up with her own commitment to The Firm. He decided he would further his investigation, but until then, he was going to keep an eye out for Anthony.

Four

    Courtney decided to introduce Anthony as one of her street associates to Aaliyah Huffman, Ryan Reynolds, and her assistant, Kimberly. Steve Savage had unexpectedly texted her back, stating that he had a court hearing to attend and couldn't make it. They were all back in her chambers listening to Anthony talk.

    "I have partners in every borough, including the tri-states, from North Philly to the gutter streets of Newark and East Orange, all the way back down to Norfolk, Virginia. This operation we're talking about could possibly be a multi-billion-dollar monopoly. It gets no better than this if you ask me," he said, looking around at all the eyes glued to him and deciphering his every word.

    "I have a total of seventeen vacant properties spread across ten states. Also, I have over forty-three box trucks and thirty-two Sprinter vans delivering on the interstates every day, up and down the East and West Coast. I can make one call to my interior decorator, and she will have all the properties fixed up as if they were occupied. I'm pretty sure we can park a car or two in the driveways. We can also utilize each residence as a stash house. I strongly believe that with the amount of currency and drug supply we're discussing, my available resources should be a priority."

    "And it is, and thank you," Courtney said. "All in favor, say I."

    Each individual responded, "I," in favor of rolling with Anthony's proposal, all except for Steve Savage. Regardless of his vote, the majority rules.

    "Anthony, I would like for you and Ryan to get together and figure out how you're going to distribute the drug supply to the street-level dealers in every state and city mentioned,"

Courtney said. "That way, when Ryan draws up the warrants and indictments, we know exactly what and who we're going for. It won't be any confusion. Rule number one...we keep everything professional and by the book concerning the law." She made sure to give each and every one of them eye contact.

"Moving forward, our grand opening for the new firm and bondsman company should be within the next two weeks. I'm covering the loose ends on the deal as we speak. My partner, Aaliyah Huffman, has been appointed President to lead that branch. As you all know," Courtney said, looking in Aaliyah's direction, "the same rules still apply."

"Without a doubt, sis!" Aaliyah replied.

"And the Queen of Wakanda," she laughed out loud, "Natasha, she will continue to run our New Jersey front office. We're preparing to open our California law office in ninety days. I'm appointing Kimberly to run it until we begin the hiring process. Any questions?" she asked, looking down at her rose gold presidential Rolex. No one answered. "Then, this meeting is officially adjourned."

Ryan Reynolds stopped Courtney before she exited her Chambers. Just recently, he had been hearing rumors from the local jail deputies he bowls with on Sunday nights, and figured he would inform her of their conversations.

"As of lately, your name has been ringing throughout the jails. The inmates in the jail are calling you Sweet Jones."

"Sweet Jones!?" she repeated, laughing.

"Yeah, they say it's because you give out more bonds and less jail sentences than any other federal judge in the state."

"After hearing that, I was thinking we should give it a little balance and try doing it quarterly. Maybe, every ninety days, we put our foot on their necks. The last thing we need is for statements like that to make it to the Supreme Court."

"Indeed! I'm with you!" Courtney replied. "I will take what you just told me into consideration...only after I empty this metric ton container!"

Steve Savage was debriefed on the meeting held in Courtney's chambers earlier by Aaliyah Huffman. He couldn't believe the audacity of Courtney to hold a meeting without him being present

"...but she runs shit!" Aaliyah replied. "She didn't have to tell you anything, but she made sure you were updated and not left out. You should be grateful! Who the hell you supposed to be, Donald Trump? All of a sudden, I'm Zelinski? Boy boo! I could have been getting my hair and nails done, but Courtney made sure I put my business to the side. To her, making sure you were informed was more important. That's all I'm saying. Damn!! Who pissed in your lemonade today?"

"I'm sorry. It's just been hectic all day today," he said as he walked out of Aliyah's office.

Natasha was no snoop. In fact, she was living in the lap of luxury. She was Natasha Bryant, the famous attorney at law. She posed for pictures and attended New York Knicks and Yankees baseball games. She was even spotted on the red carpet at the Grammy Awards. Natasha was doing everything that Courtney expected her to do. Being so busy kept her oblivious to the matrix actually happening around her. The intent was not to keep The Firm away from her. It served more as a security measure. The less she knew, the better.

Natasha was a law-abiding, practicing attorney. Once she received the green light to begin hiring attorneys, she wasted no time. In her first two weeks, she hired two paralegals and two lawyers. The Queen of Wakanda was finally marking her own territory. That was the end goal for each law firm and joint venture. Natasha would often check in with Courtney. In return, Courtney would often tell her that she was doing a wonderful job.

Kandy had finally gotten the chance to catch back up with her sister, Courtney. Their busy schedules kept them from their usual girl trips and frequent house visits. After flying twenty-one hours in her private G6 Lear, Kandy finally landed safely from Cape Town, South Africa, to JFK International Airport. Courtney could not wait to tell her about her date

"Girl! Anthony took me on the helicopter, and I was like okay! Of course, we know I've ridden in one several times…I've just never been on a romantic date in one."

"So where did you fly to?" Kandy asked.

"We flew over the five boroughs in New York. From up in the air, the city and the bright lights were so beautiful. We even circled the Statue of Liberty twice and flew over the Brooklyn Bridge."

"Aww! Sounds like you had a good time," Kandy replied.

"I'm not done yet," Courtney countered.

"I'm sorry," Kandy said, laughing.

"We drank an entire bottle of Ace of Spades and sang along to Alicia Keys and Jay-Z's song. Then suddenly, he reached over and handed me two dozen gold ribbon sky-blue roses. I got wet instantly!"

"Not the thousand-dollar-a-piece blue roses? Did he propose?"

"No, stupid! He wished me a happy birthday, and we considered it a Netflix-and-nap-cap night," Courtney replied.

"Yeah, and I bet that movie was hot and steamy too," Kandy said, laughing.

Courtney's DEA connect called and asked if they could meet soon. He said he had some vital information she would be interested in. Courtney didn't know how to respond, but she trusted the source. It was one of her most reliable, so she agreed to meet with him the following Friday.

James Cook was a special drug task force agent out of the Miami, Florida, federal district. He was a twenty-seven-year-old recently divorced man with three children, going through an ugly settlement. At the time, he had served as a high-ranking DEA federal agent for several years. His attorney informed him that his ex-wife, Ciara Cook, would be receiving monthly spousal support due to his infidelity. The amount totaled more than half of his eighty-five-thousand-dollar annual pension. She would also be awarded their beautiful two-story, five-bedroom estate, his pit bull bully, Capone, and one of their two vehicle, including his 2024 Cadillac truck. The judge ruled it was more suitable for a family of four.

Ciara didn't spare the rod. She drained James for everything he had worked so hard to attain, leaving him emotionally scarred, depressed, and homeless with only a 2001 Nissan Altima and five hundred dollars to his name.

One day, James walked into his superior's front office to ask for help. He needed either a payday loan or a raise due to his situation. He explained that he had been sleeping in his car and barely had money to eat. His captain looked him in the eyes and said, "It sounds like an unfortunate situation. I can get with the rest of the task force, and we can start you a GoFundMe."

He then reached into his back pocket to retrieve his wallet. Just from looking, James counted over seven crisp one-hundred-dollar bills. His captain fiddled through them and handed him a single twenty-dollar bill.

James couldn't believe what had just happened. *Were these the same people he risked his life for every day on the beat?* He brought in millions in guns and drugs annually, yet they couldn't even offer an advance on his pay. That day changed his entire perspective on law enforcement. He realized they could care less about him as a human being. To them, he was just another puppet in a white man's puppet show. He walked out of the captain's office and was never the same again.

In 2024, James Cook was introduced to Courtney through Kandy. Life had gotten the best of him and he was strongly contemplating taking his life when he returned home. That's when he spotted and pulled over a burgundy Lamborghini truck, driving without a license plate, and headed towards the Miami district.

Kandy was on her way to pay one of her top shootas, Don Juan, for his services when Agent Cook pulled her over. After smelling the blueberry marijuana reeking from her vehicle, he detained her and proceeded to search the vehicle. Upon further investigation, he discovered that she had half a pound of marijuana and an undisclosed amount of cash money in her possession, which was a felony.

He read Kandy her Miranda rights, and placed her under arrest. While sitting in his squad car and doing his paperwork, she asked if she could talk to him?

"Of course," he replied, while he continued typing his paperwork.

"Look! I've only driven that truck once or twice. It's paid for in full and has less than a thousand miles on it. The title is in the glove compartment. If you release me, it's all yours. No harm, no foul! You walk away with a three-hundred-thousand-dollar car and two duffel bags full of cash. For your bonus, since you're a handsome man, I'll give you some of this cookie." She spread her legs open and gave him an intense, seductive look.

No Black man walking God's green earth would have turned down a deal of that magnitude. He instantly stopped typing, turned around, and looked at her beautiful face.

"You better not be lying to me."

"You would be a fool not to take this deal because I can guarantee you will not meet a rich freaky slut like me who is down for whatever and will let you have your way with her."

Two Weeks Later

James drove up in his Lamborghini truck to meet back up with Kandy. This time they were discussing drug supply, money, and the cartel. He and Kandy had become close associates and business partners. They shook hands and made plans to do a lot of deals in the near future. Kandy pissed money and often drove foreign cars once and gave them away. Ever since she was a teenager, she knew how to use her sex appeal to get whatever she wanted in life.

Agent James Cook met up with Courtney at a local car wash in East Orange, New Jersey. He was already there when she arrived in a blue, newer model Yukon Denali. He exited his rental and entered.

"Good evening," he said.

"Evening," she replied.

"I received some information from a few of my colleagues that the shipment you had picked up was not the correct one."

"Elaborate," she said, pulling down her designer Dior frames.

"The shipment you received had a fentanyl mix of fifteen-point nine percent in each single kilo."

"I don't understand where you are going with this," Courtney said, looking confused.

"What I am saying, boss, is that there is enough fentanyl in each kilo to kill a mature elephant. Only God knows how many people can and will die if that supply gets distributed. That is why the government wanted it destroyed immediately."

"I have already begun the process, and the supply has been delivered to at least ten states. As of right now, they have already begun distributing it to the local street dealers. James, how the hell did this happen?"

"I am just getting this information now," he replied. "Your original container was scheduled to be picked up at the Customs Pier and not the Boston loading dock. Somehow something went wrong, and that entire play got mixed up."

"I do recall meeting up with Ryan Reynolds about that specific location being rerouted, but since we received the load, I did not think much of it. What do you think I should do?"

"I honestly believe you should call it off and have as much of that product taken off the streets and destroyed as soon as possible. It is not worth the risk," James said, looking in Courtney's direction as she sat emotionless, staring out of the window.

"I spent a lot of money on this metric ton. So, who is going to pay me back my damn money?"

James knew she was just thinking out loud. He had done his job perfectly and he knew Courtney was damn near a billionaire. There was no way she was really stressing over money.

"But it's going to open up an entire federal investigation once these bodies begin dropping," he said.

"Them crack fiends wanted that potent smack anyways, so who the hell cares!" she yelled back, frustrated.

"The government!" he replied.

"I have too much invested, James. I'll have my lieutenants in each state cut the coke with more baking soda. I'm not pulling back on this operation. It's a go! I'll keep in touch," she said before pulling away.

James stood in the middle of the street, shaking his head. He knew the consequences and repercussions that were ahead if she was content with putting the supply on the streets. He realized that was his sign to get out of the game before the dead bodies began popping up statewide.

After trying to reach Anthony several times, Courtney called her sister Kandy to tell her the play and maybe get a second opinion.

"Hey! What's up, sis?" Kandy said, answering her phone.

"Hey!" Courtney replied. "I need some advice without you patronizing me," she said.

"Whatever. Shoot it to me," Kandy said.

"I purchased an MT for fifty dollars, and it came back with Tylenol mixed in it."

She was actually speaking in code, but Kandy knew exactly what she was talking about.

"First of all, fifty for an MT is way too cheap. The only way you would get it that cheap is if the product was tainted or poisoned with Tylenol. Did you personally purchase the MT?" Kandy asked.

"No, I sent Steve to purchase it. Now that we're talking about it, I recall him saying something about a drought and us cutting the product," Courtney replied.

"From what I'm hearing, I'm thinking Steve purchased the tainted container for twenty on purpose so he could pocket thirty. I don't see any other reason why he would even purchase it. Sis, you really don't want to sell that shit. You have to be careful with them tainted containers. They seriously bring unwarranted attention. I know you're probably upset right now, but it's only money. Wins and losses come with being bosses. Don't let this small feat knock you off your podium. You got this."

"No doubt," Courtney replied. "But the product has already hit the streets. We'll just have to wait and see."

An emergency meeting was texted to every member of The Firm's email and regular text messages. They were each told to report to Courtney's luxurious estate by 7 pm the following day.

The next day, upon arriving, she recognized that her driveway wasn't just filled with several of her own foreign vehicles, the remainder belonged to The Firm. She glanced and surveyed the driveway to see who had already arrived, and from her presumption, everyone was present.

Courtney exited her Maybach with another woman. They both entered her beautiful estate and began walking down the long South Wing corridor before entering the Great Room. Her staff noticed that she was completely dressed down, wearing a Fear of God hoodie and jean outfit, a pair of wheat Timberlands, and her signature Dior designer shades. The woman by her side quickly took a seat without saying anything. She didn't even greet everyone like always. Her energy was different. She just began talking.

"It seems as if there was a mix-up or some sort of miscommunication with this metric ton we just purchased. I've been informed of the pros and cons of this unfortunate situation, and I plan on handling it accordingly. Moreover, my question to you all is, does anyone know why we purchased a tainted container, and from the wrong port at that?"

Steve Savage stood up. "Courtney, I take full responsibility because I didn't do my own research before I purchased the container. It just came to me as a cheap container full of cocaine. I'm thinking since it's a drought. We could jump on it and stretch it however we needed to gain the most efficient profit. I purchased it for twenty-five million.

Our budget was fifty, with plans on stretching it due to the drought. I estimated it to bring in a billion dollars."

"And what did you do with the other twenty-five million?" she asked, standing with her hands on her thick hips.

He went into his wallet and passed the paper bank receipt over to Courtney. It read that a deposit of twenty-five million dollars and zero cents was deposited into her business's account. She looked at the date and time. It was, in fact, two weeks ago. The time was 8 am. *Just after the purchase that went down around six,* she thought while reading it.

"I stopped past the office and gave it to Aaliyah big head ass! She kept the copy, and I left with the original the same day," he replied, looking at both her and Aaliyah with a sour face.

She could tell he was feeling some type of way. It took everything in her not to smile. She had to keep everything professional. Steve was a multimillionaire and was one of her highly compensated workers. He knew not to steal from her.

Courtney looked back at the woman sitting in the chair and waved her over, signaling for her to join in. She stood up, walked over, and without an introduction, began speaking. "I believe you one hundred percent. I've been a victim of a tainted container I purchased, and it wasn't pleasant. I witnessed people dying faster than the COVID pandemic, and it was at a rapid rate. The government is always behind the tainted container sales."

"That's crazy," someone in the room chimed in.

"But why?" Kimberly asked.

"Why would they destroy them when they can sell them on the black web or back to the drug cartels for multi-millions of dollars? It's just a different form of how they hustle, manipulate, and control the population. It's always risky. Do note, there is no honor amongst thieves. Nor is there a right way to do the wrong thing. Don't allow this drug underworld to sink you deep into its abyss or pull the wool over your eyes." She looked over at Courtney while making that particular statement.

"Everything that glitters is not gold. You just have to always outthink your opponent before you make your next business decision. Often, when containers of this magnitude hit the streets, the bodies do too. So, why am I here...you may all be thinking. I have a contentious plan to stamp the product as if it came from an overseas cartel instead of the United States. Word of mouth is always and will forever be the best form of communication. I'm going to need each of you to contact every street-level pusher and dealer in every state and inform them that the product their selling is called Red Death Scorpion and inform them that it's very potent." She gave them all a serious look.

"Let them know it derived from the Mexican Cartel and that it is vital that they cut it with a five...nothing less. That's the only way we're going to be able to slow down the death rate and still bring in the profits. The odds are against us. Right now, we're just trying to prevent another Walking Dead disaster. The end result is that the drug supply will be stamped, and all the dealers know. This specific batch could be deadly, and most of all is cartel related. The overall goal is to keep your name far away from any and all narcotics being dealt while still making some money. It's been personally done by me, so I know it works. Thank you for your time. I know you all have work to get to!"

Kandy walked over and hugged her sister, wishing her well before exiting the meeting.

Steve Savage was back at his New York Condominium looking over some recent video footage. He'd been missing out on The Firm's meetings because he was often putting in man-hours following Courtney and Anthony around the city. After finally arriving to Anthony's residence, he began plotting out his mission. *It's only going to be within a matter of time*, he thought, looking down at his Rolex. He retrieved his phone from his Polo jacket and called Ryan Reynolds.

"Hello!" he answered.

"Can you talk?" Steve asked.

Ryan was actually sound asleep in bed with his wife, but he decided to get up to see why Steve Savage was calling him at 3 am. Once he stepped onto his balcony, he closed the sliding door behind him.

"Okay, I can talk now," he said.

"Remember when I told you I was going to need that favor you owe me?" Steve asked.

"I remember," Ryan replied, shaking his head, knowing Steve was up to one of his devious attacks again.

Steve had leverage on him that could destroy his relationship with Courtney and The Firm. He was more than ready to finally get that dark cloud of extortion from over his head. "Okay, so what do you need me to do?" he asked.

One Friday evening, Steve Savage was at the courthouse testifying in a drug case on behalf of the Federal Government. After his court proceedings ended, he decided to stop by Ryan Reynolds' District Attorney's office on the third floor to see if he was available to overlook a few drug indictments and have them signed by the judge. He was taken aback when he walked up and overheard Ryan having a conversation with two DEA agents about Courtney and The Firm. He couldn't believe what he was hearing through the cracked office door. Without hesitation, he pulled out his iPhone and began recording Ryan's entire five-minute conversation.

Steve Savage had just uncovered that Ryan was a mole placed to infiltrate The Firm. The video and audio were crystal clear. It showed him standing up and revealing their secret codes and meetings to his two colleagues. From listening, Steve could tell Ryan didn't have enough solid evidence to convict her, yet, but he believed it was only a matter of time.

"I'm planning on setting up the boss lady's boy toy with enough coke and guns to put his ass under the jail, but I'm going to need you to do your part," Steve said.

Ryan disagreed. "You know there's no way we're going to be able to get away with that."

"Of course we will," Steve replied nonchalantly. "I'm pretty sure a man as smart as you will figure it out. I'll be calling you back in a couple of days," he said before ending the call.

Natasha was on her lunch break when she was suddenly approached by a fellow friend and colleague of hers, April "The Hammer" Johnson, a well-known and feared name in the federal court system. She was known for her sharp tactics and tough sentences. April also headed the Federal District Attorney's Office of New Jersey. She and Natasha had been introduced at the Potter's House Ministry through their mothers, Carolyn and Wanda, who both held key positions there.

Just recently, they had attended April's eldest sister, Mercedes' beautiful wedding in Jamaica. It was there that Natasha caught the bouquet and took pictures with April, along with the bride and groom.

"Hey girl! How you been?" April asked.

"Blessed and highly favored," Natasha confidently said.

"Amen to that!" April replied.

"And yourself?" Natasha asked.

"Working, working, and working some more." They both burst out laughing. "This profession can be mentally strenuous at times," April said while drinking her Starbucks iced coffee.

"Yes indeed," Natasha agreed. "But we do it because we love it."

April had been keeping tabs on Natasha ever since she joined Courtney, Bryant, Huffman, and Associates. She knew of Courtney, but she kept her distance, especially at the courthouse. Most of the time, if any of her clients' cases were scheduled to be held in Courtney's courtroom, she would request a continuance in hopes that another sitting judge would accept the case on their docket. In all of her fifteen years as a respected Chief Prosecutor, she had yet to win a single high-profile case in Courtney's courtroom.

Courtney Jones had a reputation that didn't flow too well with her. She always felt the corruption and extortion vibes whenever she entered her courtroom. She felt the need to inform Natasha because she wasn't just any ordinary colleague, she was indeed her friend.

Aaliyah so happened to be meeting up with a client to discuss the recent plea bargain she negotiated when she suddenly spotted the two women sitting at the table together. She knew of April very well, but she didn't have a clue that she and Natasha also knew one another. She sat patiently for a couple of minutes and watched their body language.

From her observation, they did more laughing than anything. As far as she was concerned, April was stern, distant, by the book, and didn't correspond or would even make plea deals with their law firm. She thought that this could be a gift or a curse. Either way, she had some investigating to do. Aaliyah ordered her food to go and left the food court immediately!

"First and for most congratulations on The Firm, April said.

"Thank you," Natasha replied. "You know, I've been working in the court system for over a decade, and I haven't seen a law firm so successful."

"Question?" April asked. "Have you ever wondered why, out of the hundreds of cases on the dockets, we've never been on a case together?

"I have," Natasha replied, "but you are allotting to something, so what is it?"

April took another sip of her iced coffee and whispered,

"I have reason to believe that your law firm is corrupt. I can't prove it, but I've been around long enough to see and put things together. I've also begun an open investigation myself, The minute I get enough evidence, I plan on taking Courtney Jones and all of her colleagues with her down, so I urge you to get out before it's too late."

"Wow! That's one hell of an accusation," Natasha added.

"You do know that I am the lead partner at Courtney, Bryant, Huffman, and Associates?"

"Of course, but that's just a title. You still answer to Courtney Jones, correct?"

Natasha didn't like her comment, but in truth, it was accurate.

"Yes, I do," Natasha replied.

"Just think about what I'm telling you because I'm not the only one who knows she's corrupt. A few of my district attorney colleagues are suspected of working in cahoots with her and are currently under investigation by internal affairs. I received the memo through a trusted source. I'm just giving it to you the way it was given to me. To know is to be aware. The rest is up to you, my friend," she said before getting up and walking away.

Moments later, Natasha called out to her, stopping her in her tracks. April turned around, and Natasha thanked her. April nodded and smiled before she continued walking.

Dead bodies were popping up in the New York and New Jersey districts. So far, the death toll had increased and was estimated to be around 200 and rising. The new drug, Red Death Scorpion, was a fentanyl-based killer sweeping the city streets.

"I'll be reporting exclusively on this story tonight at six. The Sinaloa Cartel has claimed responsibility. I'm Sara McCallum reporting live on your side from WGN News Eight."

Courtney and Aaliyah sat in the back of her Maybach and made a toast. They loved it when a plan came together.

"I don't want to spoil our celebration, but I have something to tell you," Aaliyah said.

Whenever Courtney was serious, she would remove her Chanel designer shades, revealing her natural light hazel eyes. She didn't like Aaliyah's tone at all. After Aaliyah finished telling her about the meeting she had witnessed, Courtney went into deep thought.

"If it's not one thing, it's another," she said aloud.

She had just climbed over one hurdle, and now here came another. There was no telling what they had been discussing, but she was sharp enough to know that April was definitely a problem. In fact, she had documentation of April forwarding hundreds of her case files to another judge. Whatever the case, she knew she needed to move cautiously around The Firm until she had a chance to pick Natasha's brain. She liked Natasha a lot, but before she let her bring down her entire operation, she would kill her dead. As for April Johnson...she was also on her hit list. It was only a matter of time.

Agent James Cook arrived at his multimillion-dollar luxury estate in Belize. He decided to lay low and live out the rest of his days in the lap of luxury. He stood barefoot on his cream and caramel-colored marble floor, staring at his reflection. He had spent millions on reconstructing his identity. His new beard and facial features were so unrecognizable that he could barely recognize himself. Between Kandy and her sister, Courtney, he estimated he had made over one hundred and fifty million dollars, and he was determined to enjoy every cent of it.

He logged into his email several times and noticed that Courtney had called him but he had already decided that chapter of his life was completely over. He didn't even bother to entertain her messages. There was simply no need to. He erased them all while lighting his Cuban cigar. He opened his back door and stepped out onto the white sandy beach. Dressed in white linen pants, a button-up polo, Polo boat slippers, and a pair of white and gold designer Cartier frames, he took in the peaceful view. For him, life couldn't have been better. He was determined to never look back. *It's clearly full sail ahead from here,* he thought, gazing out into the big blue ocean.

A million miles away in her luxury penthouse, Natasha Bryant was feeling the same. Looking around, she could've never have imagined living her life so lavishly. In the back of her mind, she always wondered how Courtney could afford such a lifestyle. After having the conversation with April Johnson, everything was beginning to make sense. She looked around and admired her elegant palace. Without a doubt, she knew it would have taken her another fifteen to twenty years of handling caseloads to even dream of owning a penthouse of this magnitude. To think, Courtney had given it away like an old pair of stilettos, along with the added amenities such as the luxury vehicle and chauffeur. She loved her lifestyle and career. There was just no way she could see herself going back to a regular life. This life was surreal, fantastic, and quite amazing.

⚜

Anthony was awakened around 5 am by loud banging at his front door. He jumped up and looked out his bedroom window, only to see that his entire estate was surrounded by law enforcement. Without hesitation, he hurried downstairs to open his fifty-thousand-dollar cherry oakwood door. He was already upset that the police were knocking on his door with their flashlights. As soon as he opened the door, several DEA and FBI agents stood flashing their badges and presented a search warrant as they entered his residence.

"Who sanctioned this raid?" Anthony asked.

The agents began ransacking his estate without another word. Anthony just sat down, shaking his head. He knew he was clean. It would only be a matter of time before they ended up uncuffing him and apologizing. He knew too many head honchos in law enforcement and down at the Federal Bureau. One call would put an end to all of this.

Moments later, agents began walking past him with trash bags filled with, what they claimed, was evidence. He couldn't imagine having anything illegal in his residence. *What the hell is in those bags,* he thought to himself. He continued sitting quietly until he was eventually read his rights and arrested. As he was escorted to the police cruiser, news reporters stood just a few feet away, along with a small crowd of onlookers.

Two hours later, Anthony was informed of his attorney's visit. He was taken down to the visitation room, where he saw Aaliyah Huffman, but she wasn't alone. He was surprised to see her sitting beside his ex-girlfriend and long-time trusted assistant, Michelle. They both took a seat and pulled out his file, thick with felonies, before she began talking.

Ten Years Earlier

Anthony and Slim were among the elite. They had spread their drug and sex empire through several states. Slim found out through a trusted source that Anthony had been speaking to his cartel connect behind his back. When Slim confronted Anthony, he looked him dead in the face and denied the allegation.

"Youngin', we've made millions together. I took you off the streets and treated you like a son. This is how you thank me? By going behind my back and renegotiating business deals without my knowledge?"

Anthony had, in fact, done exactly that. He was tired of Slim's old-school hustling tactics. The world was evolving and moving at a faster pace. Slim seemed content to settle for what they already had. Anthony wanted to expand the business. He had planned to tell Slim once the money started flowing in, but Slim found out before he could explain. Slim took it as a sign of disloyalty and decided to part ways.

Anthony couldn't allow that to happen. He had too many people depending on him. His multimillion-dollar empire was crumbling right before his eyes. He begged and pleaded with Slim to reconsider, but to no avail. Slim asked him to leave his hotel room and to make sure he left what he owed. Anthony stormed out and returned to his own hotel room. He paced the floor while smoking a Newport. If he were to wire Slim the two million dollars, it would leave him in a bind. He wouldn't be able to pay the connect for the next shipment. So, he needed a stall tactic and he needed it fast. He left and returned to Slim's room.

Upon entering, he noticed Slim wasn't alone. "I'll come back later," he said.

Slim didn't take it well. Two large men blocked him from leaving. Normally, he'd carry his gun, but there was no need for it when he was only visiting Slim.

That was his mistake.

Slim told him to wire the money immediately.

"I just need a couple of days, Slim," Anthony pleaded.

"I'm giving you a couple of minutes," Slim replied.

Slim had been Anthony's main source of income for the past decade. He knew exactly how much money Anthony should have had in his account, but Anthony lived a lifestyle well beyond his means. Instead of profiting from the business, he survived on Slim's consignments. His account would have been in the negative if he had sent the two million. He decided he'd take whatever punishment Slim had for him. He couldn't afford to give him his last.

This wasn't the first time he had come up short. He figured Slim might cut him off for a month or two, but that would give him just enough time to buy a new supply and triple the profit. He even planned to pay Slim back with interest.

By the time Anthony regained consciousness, eight hours had passed. The squeaky sound of the maids pushing carts outside the hotel room woke him. He was in excruciating pain and realized immediately that he was lying in a pool of his own blood. Once he understood where he was, he crawled to the bathroom. He used the sink to pull himself to his feet. When he looked into the mirror, he cried out in anguish.

He couldn't even recognize the face looking back at him. His head was swollen like a watermelon, his eyes were both black and swollen shut, his bottom lip was almost ripped off of his face, and both of his front teeth were missing. He had been severely beaten, and left for dead. He needed medical attention right away. He reached for the towel folded on top of the counter and covered his entire head, while exiting the room.

After two months, he had gone through several surgeries and reconstructions. In all, there were two hundred staples and stitches applied to his head, lip, and upper eye. Anthony was finally discharged from Chesapeake General Hospital. He decided to stay at his girlfriend, Michelle's, apartment until he was completely healed. He knew and understood what he'd done was foul, but he didn't deserve to get beaten like this. He looked at Slim like a father figure and wouldn't have even thought he would allow something like this to happen to him, but he did. From that point, Anthony knew their relationship would never be the same.

He was finally able to go out in public when he and Michelle were entering his vehicle. A black Cadillac truck pulled up and blocked them in. Anthony recognized the vehicle immediately–it belonged to Slim. Anthony exited his vehicle and walked up to the truck. The back passenger's tinted window rolled down. Slim sat there smoking a Cuban cigar.

"I'm glad to see you survived that one. Now, you have twenty-four hours to get my money, or you'll be visiting that hospital again before they can change the sheets on your bed," Slim said. He rolled up his window and instructed his driver to pull away.

Anthony stood there in shock. He knew there was only one way out of this lifestyle, and it was death. When he got back into his girlfriend's vehicle, he told her, "I'm going to murder Slim by the end of the day."

Anthony looked at both women, confused. "But how do you two know one another?" he asked.

"Oh, her?" Aaliyah said. "That's an old friend of mine. We go way back. When she found the attorney for your son, she was actually looking for me. I just so happened to be working for Courtney when she looked us up on our website. Small world, right?" she said casually.

"But to hell with the meet and greet, Courtney has been informed that you are the person responsible for the murder of her father, while also bringing down an international drug empire. If you were a cop, you'd be getting a Purple Heart or something, but since you're part of the underworld, that my friend, is one serious violation. We're all connected when you think about it. You almost got away with it," Aaliyah said, looking to her right at her star witness – the one person Anthony was a hundred percent sure he had told that he killed Slim. She became jealous and bitter when he just up and decided to leave her for Courtney.

"You are charged with a boatload of felonies. Just maybe, I can work out a plea bargain for 25 years. You'll end up doing eighteen. That's my only and final offer. Consider this a gift from Courtney. For the record, the District Attorney has no clue about your involvement in Slim's murder...yet." She passed him a photo of the murder weapon recovered at one of his properties.

"In order to keep it that way, I'm going to need you to sign over everything you own. Your businesses, homes, cars, investments, stocks, CD accounts, including your Swiss bank account. Michelle knows everything, so if you dare hold back any information, I promise you, Courtney will make sure your ass is under the prison for life."

"I had no clue Slim was Courtney's father. I felt it was either him or me," Anthony tried to explain, but it was as if he were talking to a wall.

The two women carried on a conversation right in front of him. He couldn't believe Michelle... of all people. She knew he was only defending himself and didn't vouch for him at all. He shook his head because he was so disappointed in her.

Once they finished their conversation, Aaliyah passed Anthony his felony charges, and his mouth dropped. He was charged with possession with intent to distribute twenty kilos of Red Death Scorpion fentanyl-based cocaine, having several AK-47 assault weapons, and having quarter million dollars in street cash. All tens, fifties, and five-dollar bills.

"This some grimy shit," he said, knowing that was an automatic conviction.

Courtney had tricked him. She never wanted to partner up. She wanted his empire the entire time. He didn't see this coming at all. He knew she had him. He didn't have a choice. So, he began signing the plea bargain.

Courtney received the email that the plea was signed and sealed. She smiled while placing her iPhone back into her crocodile Birkin designer bag. She did, in fact, want to partner with Anthony, but after finding out that he was the person responsible for killing her father, Slim, all bets were off the table.

Even though she and Slim never had a father-daughter relationship, he was still her father. Plus, Anthony had a lot more going on than what he had revealed to her. Instead of trying to figure him out, it was easier to take his fortune and send him to prison.

Courtney was climbing the cartel ladder and was now among the top five drug lords on the East Coast. She was becoming more powerful than she could have ever imagined.

Five

The United States Federal Courthouse was busy as always. Judge Courtney Jones's docket wasn't as loaded with ICE cases and deportations. Today, she was mostly proceeding with narcotics cases. District Attorney April Johnson had two drug cases in Courtney's courtroom. She needed the judge to revoke the federal bond because the defendant was deemed a flight risk and had already been arrested by the federal fugitive task force, but it was as if she were talking to a bale of hay. Judge Courtney Jones never looked her in the eye once and freely granted the defendant bond. Then, she scheduled another court date for his preliminary hearing.

April stood in shock. It was unbelievable what she had just witnessed. Then again, she knew she would never win a case in Judge Jones's courtroom, today or in the foreseeable future. She had planned to file a complaint with the United States Bar Association as soon as she returned to the DA's office.

April Johnson was exiting the federal courthouse parking lot around 5:30 pm when she quickly noticed a black vehicle tailing her. A wave of paranoia kicked in until she recognized it was the luxury Maybach belonging to Judge Courtney Jones.

But why would she be following her?

She just continued to drive for the next several blocks until she approached the red light near a busy intersection. Suddenly, the Maybach pulled up beside her Lexus. She was expecting the window to roll down, but it didn't. One minute later, the stoplight changed, and the vehicle drove away.

April's intuition told her that Courtney Jones was sitting on the other side of the dark-tinted window, staring directly at her. She still had the goose bumps running down her arms. It was another form of power that Courtney was demonstrating, and April received her message loud and clear. She knew it was time to gather up all of the piled-up evidence she had against Courtney and her crooked law firm. For some strange reason, she felt that Courtney knew that she was on to her.

⚜

    Courtney was back at her luxury estate when Warren, the head of her security, walked in with information he had discovered on the security system that he thought she might want to see. A few minutes later, she rose from her rug, after performing her Salat prayer, and followed him back to her security room downstairs.

    The footage she was shown didn't even surprise her. She watched as she exited her bedroom, leaving Anthony alone. The video showed her iPhone on the nightstand vibrating. She watched as he rose from out of the covers, while looking to see if the coast was clear, before he began reading the sent message. Shortly after, he began texting something back into her phone. Her security team did a thorough investigation of pulling up old and erased messages from her iPhone.

    According to the date and time, it revealed that Courtney had received a text message around 12:37 pm asking her to send over her account numbers. Anthony read the message, and at 12:38, he sent both his account and routing numbers back to the anonymous source. Then, he erased the message from her phone. He hadn't realized it yet, but that was a payment of sixty million dollars.

    Courtney was pissed!! If it wasn't for the holy month of Ramadan, she would have had his head chopped completely off. She ultimately decided to call Aaliyah Huffman, and Ryan Reynolds, instructing them both to void his plea agreement. If it was up to her, he was never going to see the light of day again.

    She was now running her entire operation through the tristate and five boroughs that Anthony once ran. She used all 25 of his real estate properties along the eastern seaboard to store her overly stockpile of cash and drug supply. She and Steve Savage sat in the back of her Maybach, and she thanked him for the long man-hours he put in following Anthony until he could confirm his residence.

"Anything for you, Courtney" he said with the googly eyes.

She had always known he was a sucker for her, and right at this moment, she needed to relieve some tension. She took three shots of tequila and drank two full glasses of red wine before pulling her skirt up past her waist. She kissed him on his lips while instructing him to make her feel good. Then, she proceeded to push his head down as she lay back and closed her eyes.

Courtney was back home when she received a call from Natasha Bryant asking her to turn on News 8 immediately. As soon as she did, she observed the Mayor of New Jersey standing and talking by the podium. Alongside him were the commissioner of the police department and the head District Attorney, April Johnson.

"We are here to bring forth corruption, bribery, extortion, and murder in the first-degree indictments against Judge Courtney Jones. She has used her power of liberty, justice, and freedom to bestow pain, corruption, and disruption within our court system. We will continue to do a thorough investigation according to these allegations."

April Johnson stepped up to the podium.

"We have reason to believe that the judge is allegedly nothing more than a psychopathic, cartel drug supplier, mass manipulator, who has bamboozled her way throughout her career as a sitting officer of the courts. Allegedly, she is responsible for shipping metric tons of cocaine throughout the tri-state.

Courtney had seen enough. She jumped up and ran to retrieve her phone. She knew her freedom was limited, and she knew the system well enough and understood that, as soon as the warrants and indictments were signed, the Feds were coming. Without any further hesitation, she called her most trusted friend, Aaliyah Huffman, but she didn't answer. Courtney just remembered, Aaliyah and a few colleagues went on a weekend yacht cruise and weren't going to have any service until Monday.

Then, she called Kandy on WhatsApp, but she was ten thousand miles away back in Africa. Courtney's service just continued to drop.

"DAMN!!" she screamed at the top of her lungs and kicked over her nightstand.

She had no choice and went against her intuition. She called Natasha Bryant back and gave her all her routing and account numbers. She also instructed her to reroute several of her Swiss bank accounts to her sister's account. Then, she provided her with all the passwords to her iPad and the law firm's computers. She instructed Natasha to log in, download all the data to her hard drive, and get rid of every device in or around the office.

"I'm on it," Natasha said before hanging up.

Courtney began doing the same thing at home. She ran around like a chicken with its head cut off, trying to find and destroy any evidence that could incriminate her or link her to the criminal enterprise. She ordered her maids and butlers to get rid of all their electronic devices, too. Around 6 pm, Courtney was at home awaiting the arrival of the Feds. She knew their routine. They would hit every residence and business she owned at the same time. As soon as her butler informed her the cops had arrived, she stood up and tossed her phone into the burning fireplace. Her butler opened the door, and a search warrant was shoved in his face. Courtney was read her rights and detained while they searched her residence. At the same time, Aaliyah's estate in New York was also being raided. Unfortunately, she hadn't been able to destroy her devices. The Feds walked out with three computers, several iPhones, and two laptops.

Ryan Reynolds turned federal witness against Courtney, but Steve Savage stood on all ten. He was arrested and charged with conspiracy, drug distribution, and corruption. Aaliyah Huffman was charged with the same thing. Courtney was booked and taken to the federal courthouse for arraignment.

She didn't even look upset. She went along with the process silently. Afterward, she was granted bond and released through the back entrance. The front of the courthouse was swarming with news reporters and onlookers holding up *NO JUSTICE, NO PEACE* signs.

Courtney knew she would have to face the press eventually, but she wasn't up for it at the moment. She was already busy working on…yet another…calculated master plan. She called her big sister. Kandy had already heard about the allegations through a mutual friend and advised Courtney to take a vacation to relax and clear her head. Courtney thought about it and agreed, but once she returned, she knew she had to get back to work. Her first court appearance was in two months, and she needed to get her ducks in a row.

Back at federal headquarters, Ryan Reynolds was granted full immunity in exchange for testifying on behalf of the United States government against Courtney Jones. He didn't hesitate to accept the deal. Courtney was informed that Ryan Reynolds had turned state's evidence. She smirked, knowing he had never stopped being a top cop. She'd only kept him close to manipulate him.

Hadn't she paid him enough to keep his mouth shut, she thought to herself. He had violated their contract, and for that alone, she was going to order his head blown off.

The law office looked like a tornado had run through it twice.

"I mean the disrespect!" Aaliyah said, standing atop scattered papers and supplies.

She knew her career as a defense attorney had finally come to an end. It would take a miracle for the firm to survive the Feds discovering their cover-ups and all the illicit payments from clients and corrupt officials. She stood staring at her law degree, which she had just taken down from the wall. *Was it all worth it,* she thought.

"It was a good ride while it lasted," she whispered while walking away.

Natasha entered the office. "My goodness, they tore this place to ruins!" Natasha said, shaking her head in disbelief. "They had me down at the federal building for over five hours, drilling the hell out of me. They kept asking me stuff I had no clue about. I eventually agreed to a lie detector test, passed it with flying colors, and was released around midnight. I couldn't wait to get to my penthouse. I was hungry, tired, and exhausted, darling."

That didn't surprise Aaliyah at all. She knew Natasha hadn't known anything. Courtney and Aaliyah had always kept their dealings private, thus leaving Natasha clueless about what was really going on behind the scenes at the firm and the courthouse. Courtney had known The Firm might one day fall under federal investigation.

"So, is it safe to say I'll be the representing attorney for the firm?" Natasha asked.

"I haven't talked to Courtney yet, but no, thank you. I'll have my own attorney soon. I'm sure she will, too. Since you worked for the firm, it's very likely the District Attorney will try to block you from representing any of us. Case #002343, Bakmen vs. United States Supreme Court. Attorney-client privilege falls under common interest. More than likely, the sitting judge will agree."

"Umm, okay!" Natasha's tone shifted.

"I see you do know case law after all, huh, Aaliyah?" Natasha asked, as if fishing for something deeper.

"I happened to study at the prestigious University of Yale. Graduated at the top of the Dean's List in 2020. It's all public info. Google me!" she said sarcastically, walking out of the office for the final time.

Aaliyah noticed something different about Natasha. She seemed rejuvenated, confident, and unusually talkative. Aaliyah knew better than to share anything legal or personal. The energy in the room had shifted. Suddenly, her intuition told her the truth – Natasha Bryant had been wearing a wire the entire time.

Cape Town, South Africa

Aaliyah and Courtney landed on Jah'me's 200-acre airstrip located on his remote island just a hundred miles north of the world-famous Madagascar River. Courtney exited the luxury Learjet, spreading her arms wide and soaking in the warm sun rays. She was amazed at how perfect the weather felt. It was just 24 hours ago that their flight had taken off from the frigid, low January temperatures in New Jersey, only to arrive in a beautiful, sunny, 75-degree tropical oasis. Several black Range Rovers awaited their arrival to collect their luggage and escort them back to the Royal Palace. This was Aaliyah's first time visiting the country, and already she could not believe what she was witnessing.

"Is that a herd of zebras and giraffes?" Aaliyah asked, pointing in their direction.

Courtney smiled and agreed. She knew that Aaliyah was in for the shock of her life. Jah'me's island was like a fun-filled, festive fantasyland. It was estimated to be around the same size as the Queen's famous Buckingham Palace in London, but it was Jah'me's influence with the architectural designers and his hiring of some of the world's most renowned stonemasons that made his palace a one-of-a-kind modern marvel.

Upon arriving, Courtney and Aaliyah were greeted and handed roses at the main entrance. Aaliyah felt as if she were visiting royalty. Everything about the experience was regal. A mini golf cart awaited them and drove them another three minutes down the long corridor that entered into the south wing of the palace.

There, Aaliyah noticed Courtney's sister, Kandy, standing alongside her ex-husband, Jah'me, better known in the United States as the Black Ghost. They were both wearing all white. Kandy wore a beautiful Chanel sundress and sandals that exposed her perfectly manicured feet. Her long, dark hair flowed past her shoulders. Jah'me sported a polo shirt, bucket hat, linen shorts, and Polo slippers. They all embraced. Aaliyah was no stranger. She had been Jah'me's lawyer when he received the blockbuster "year and a day" prison sentence, and she had also represented Kandy in multiple cases. Jah'me welcomed them to his palace.

Within moments, he excused himself and walked away with three of his servants following behind him.

Kandy looked at Courtney and said, "I thought I told you to take a vacation?"

"I did," Courtney responded.

"What's better than coming here... where I know I'll be safe while basking in the African sun on your private beach?"

Kandy could not even challenge that comment. She knew the severity of her sister's situation, and she also knew how the Feds could show up at any given time. She believed Courtney had made the right decision. They had no jurisdiction within a thousand miles of the island. This was all thanks to a treaty granted to Jah'me by the president of Africa for his philanthropy and multimillion-dollar donations to the country.

Back in the United States, Ryan Reynolds was at the federal courthouse and testifying on behalf of the government in The United States vs. Courtney Jones and Aaliyah Huffman. He nervously took the stand around ten in the morning. He scanned the crowd of onlookers, searching for Courtney's henchmen, but did not recognize anyone.

"Mr. Reynolds, you are a Drug Enforcement Agent, correct?" April Johnson asked.

"Yes," he replied.

"Let the record show that you are under oath and have been sworn in. Mr. Reynolds, how do you know the accused, Judge Jones?"

"We met through a mutual colleague," he replied.

"And who is that colleague?" she asked.

"Aaliyah," he answered.

"Aaliyah Huffman?" April Johnson asked.

"Correct," Reynolds confirmed.

"Let the court record show that our confidential informant is referring to the accused and her co-defendant, Aaliyah Huffman, attorney at law. Mr. Reynolds, can you explain to the jury what your role was while working under Judge Jones and Aaliyah Huffman's tutelage?"

"I would meet with government officials to purchase containers full of drugs and weapons that had been confiscated by the Coast Guard or Border Patrol. These were bought at a discounted rate using revenue provided by Judge Courtney Jones. I distributed the drugs to street-level dealers. I would then set up surveillance on each stash house for two weeks and have Judge Jones sign off on bogus search and seizure warrants. Within hours, we would begin our raids across the city." He let out a big sigh and continued.

"After we executed the raids, we arrested the felons and made sure our District Attorney, Steve Savage, issued million-dollar bonds regardless of their charges. We then advised them to use our bondsman company to make bail and urged them to retain representation from our prestigious law firm, Courtney, Bryant, and Huffman...a firm known for winning drug cases. We would then split the confiscated cash profits three ways. The drugs and guns we recovered as 'evidence' were placed back into the streets. This allowed dealers to resell them. Then, we repeated this process over and over again."

Gasps of "*OOHS*" and "*AWES*" rippled through the grand jury.

"Sounds like Judge Courtney Jones was basically running a drug Ponzi scheme?" April Johnson said.

"I wouldn't call it that," Reynolds replied.

"Then elaborate for the jury," she said.

"Judge Jones was a capitalist. She ran a monopoly of business ventures off the backs of federal and corrupt government officials who, by the way, were the actual puppet masters flooding our cities with guns and drugs. She just recognized their formula and jumped on the money train."

"Allegedly," Judge Moricet interjected.

"And Aaliyah Huffman? What was her involvement?" April Johnson asked.

"She was second in command. The enforcer," he replied.

"She made sure everything went as planned and that the drugs and guns were distributed on schedule."

"Mr. Reynolds, you have spit in the face of the justice system. You took an oath and swore to protect and serve, and you did the complete opposite. It's unfortunate you're not going to jail, but it's people like you who deserve to rot in prison—not the street-level dealers," she said during her closing argument.

Judge Moricet looked over at Ryan Reynolds and asked if he had anything else to say.

"Your Honor, I busted my ass since day one for the shield. In the police academy, I experienced systemic racism. No matter how well I did in the field or in the classroom, I wasn't allowed to make rank. As a rookie on the force, I saw corruption at an all-time high. My entire precinct was racist and corrupt. Since we're putting it all on the table, I was set up by my own precinct. I was accused of stealing kilos of cocaine in my third week on the force. Now picture that. But is that in my file? No! Because it was mysteriously swept under the rug, just like everything else."

He took a pause, shook his head, and continued. "This kind of corruption has been happening long before me and my co-defendants. What we're seeing is just the tip of the iceberg. The real criminals are the government officials, mayors, and judges. That's being proven right now. Like I said, it didn't start with Judge Jones, and it won't stop with her. Like always, someone has to take one for the team. Why not the Blacks?"

The entire courtroom sat in complete silence. The information was shocking to the average tax-paying, middle-class citizen. The jury knew he had no reason to lie. He had already lost his career. His testimony gave them deeper insight into the upcoming trial against Courtney Jones and Aaliyah Huffman.

"Let the record state that Officer Ryan Reynolds has given his testimony, full cooperation, and efficient evidence allowing the United States Federal Courts to uphold the law and pursue conviction to the fullest, with liberty and justice," the judge announced. "Also, let the record show that Mr. Reynolds has been awarded complete immunity for his testimony." The judge struck his gavel, dismissing the jurors.

Five hours later, Ryan Reynolds exited through the back of the courthouse.

Unemployed, but a free man.

Natasha stood between her black and burgundy Mercedes-Benz Maybach, wearing a mini skirt, designer Chanel sunglasses, and over a million dollars in platinum and diamonds. She wore a mink trench coat and Chanel red-bottom stilettos. Her forty-eighth birthday was in a week, and she had plans to go out with a blast. She had sent out invites on Instagram and Facebook to each and every one of her friends and colleagues, reminding them that it was a themed event.

The theme was the late '80s to early '90s. She wanted all attendees to dress to impress. Her birthday bash was set to take place at the beautiful Riverdale Convention Center – it was rumored that the hourly rental rate started at ten thousand dollars an hour. Natasha wanted her followers to know she had the building locked down from eleven until four in the morning. Her post even read, "It's turn-up season."

Courtney had an epiphany while getting her pedicure. She had been so busy trying to get away from the chaos back in the States that she completely forgot about the money she had asked Natasha to wire to her sister a couple of weeks ago. She quickly rose from the table without getting another nail painted. She dashed back into the Royal Palace and ordered the first servant she saw to get her sister Kandy immediately. Minutes later, Kandy arrived with her hair half-braided.

"Gurlllll... the way UmBoomKoom Fly-eating ass came and got me, this has to be an emergency," Kandy said, walking up.

Courtney would usually laugh at Kandy's outlandish comments. She was good at making up random names for the African servants who worked around the palace, but this was by no means a joking moment. She did make a mental note to laugh at that comment later, though.

"Did Natasha ever transfer the money from my account to yours?" Courtney asked.

"I have no clue what you're talking about," Kandy said, pulling her iPhone from her back pocket. "I can check, though. It's been a while since I've had any email alerts from my bank about deposits. Did you give her the correct account and routing numbers?" she asked.

"I sure did," Courtney replied. "You know I don't play when it comes to my bag, sis."

Kandy stood silently while strolling through several bank accounts before asking, "How much was it supposed to be?"

"Two hundred and fifty million," Courtney replied.

Kandy paused mid-chew and pulled down her designer Prada sunglasses. She always did that when she was serious. "You need to check on that and see what the hell's holding up the process."

Courtney was livid. She couldn't believe Natasha would even play with her like that. Without another word, she dialed Natasha's number…only to get her professional voicemail. She immediately hung up and called the law office. On the second ring, Natasha picked up.

"Good morning! This is Natasha Bryant, Attorney at Law. How can I be of good service to you today?"

"Yes, great question. How about you be of great service and FedEx me my got damn money I asked you to wire two weeks ago? Have you bumped your head, trick?!"

"I'm sorry, may I ask who I'm speaking with?" Natasha replied in a sarcastic tone.

"Oh, so you want to play games, huh?" Courtney said, laughing. "You know this is right up my alley, hoe," she calmly added.

"Are you threatening me, Courtney?" Natasha asked.

"Who is Courtney? I don't recall ever telling you my name, Ms. Bryant. Just know you have twenty-four hours to have all of my money…and you better not be a penny short."

"Or what, Courtney?!" Natasha screamed into the phone.

Courtney hung up, laughing. "That bitch working for the Feds. You can't tell me different. I see I'm going to have to kill this heffa."

Kandy stood beside her sister. "I can have my girls on the next flight to New Jersey if you want," she said, looking down at Courtney, who sat with her hands covering her face, frustrated yet deep in thought.

"I'll let you know, sis," Courtney said, walking away.

Natasha didn't know that Courtney was more than just a powerful ex-judge. Courtney mingled with some of the most notorious gangsters in the city. Not to mention, her sister Kandy was a certified nutcase.

Natasha had gathered information from three of Courtney's federal search and seizure warrants. The records showed that federal agents had raided three luxury estates, confiscated seven foreign vehicles, and had frozen several of The Firm's offshore accounts. If that were the case, Natasha could lie to Courtney and say she never withdrew the money in time before the Feds froze the accounts, but for some reason, she figured Courtney wouldn't believe her. All she knew was that she was willing to try her hand. If it worked out in her favor, this could be the sweetest two-hundred-and-fifty-million-dollar lick ever.

Natasha made copies of the search warrants and took pictures to send to Courtney's email. She also sent a text saying she was sorry she hadn't gotten to the bank before the Feds intervened. Courtney received the text and just erased it. She had already charged it to the game.

The question was…had Natasha?

Ryan Reynolds drove up to his mother's multimillion-dollar ranch property in Clearwater, Maryland. Her eighty-fifth birthday had been the day before. Most of the family drove down from upstate that Friday to celebrate. Ryan had so much going on with his high-profile case and local media coverage that he decided to stay low. So, he arrived Saturday morning. Just by observing the driveway, it looked like it was a packed house. He wasn't expecting any guests or family members to still be at the estate at 6 am. He had planned to be in and out without being seen or judged by his rich Republican family members.

Upon arrival, several vehicles were parked along the driveway. He noticed his sister, Sara's, van was still running. He walked up to the porch, and suddenly a strong stench pierced his nostrils. The front door was wide open. He yelled for his mother and sister the moment he entered. He covered his face with his shirt because the smell was unbearable. Flies and bugs had invaded the house like they had nested there for centuries. He knew something was dead, but refused to even think the worst.

The moment he entered the dining room, not only had all nine of his family members been shot in the head, but his mother sat at the head of the table, her eyes wide open, with what looked like a rat stuffed inside her mouth. Its long tail was the only part still hanging out.

He stood in shock and fell to his knees, crying.

The message Courtney sent was signed, sealed, and delivered. He knew that he was next.

Ryan walked out to his vehicle, retrieved his .38 Special.

Without wasting a minute, he pulled the trigger.

Six

The convention center was jam-packed. It seemed as if the entire city had shown up and showed out. The men and women were dressed to impress in their late '80s, early '90s hip-hop attire. Professional VIP valet service was provided and allowed each guest to show off their fly rides. They all pulled up in some of the latest foreign cars, Teslas, Lamborghinis, Rolls-Royce Wraiths, Bentleys, and every make and model of Mercedes-Benz you could think of and flooded the parking garage. The red carpet was also available for guests to take pictures for the upcoming Best Dressed contest.

Natasha invited some of the world's most elite entertainers, sports athletes, and movie stars. They were all people she knew through her clients or had once represented in court. She arrived around 1 am with a fleet of colorful Lamborghini trucks. She stepped out of the all-pink one with tinted windows, dressed as Mary J. Blige. Her hair was dyed blonde, she wore a Yankees fitted cap, Dior designer frames, bamboo earrings, a New York Yankees striped jersey dress, and black Timberland boots. Alongside her were her six BFFs from childhood, all dressed in tight or revealing outfits. This was her night, and she was ready to turn up. If you didn't know her before tonight, you would definitely know her after, She planned to give away not one, but two Lamborghini trucks to the male and female winners of the Best Dressed contest.

Natasha was throwing around Courtney's money like never before. The way she was blowing money fast gave BMF a whole new meaning. She felt like it was finally her time to shine. She had worked her entire life to become a boss and was now in the driver's seat. This time, she was calling the shots and there was absolutely nothing anyone could do about it.

She knew she had covered her back and crossed every T and dotted every I, legally. The money she had embezzled illegally from Courtney had already been washed several times and now sat safely in a Swiss bank account overseas. As far as she was concerned, Courtney's pretty ass would soon be somebody's girlfriend, dressed in a federal khaki Gucci outfit, rotting away with a life sentence within the next six months.

She feared nothing but being broke. From the way things were looking, that was the least of her worries. Natasha began popping bottles of champagne and started dancing to Montell Jordan's hit song This Is How We Do It as it blasted over the convention's surround sound system. She smoked hookah and vibed with her girls for the rest of the evening.

Around 1:30 am, a group of eight women walked into the convention center. Each was dressed in early '90s Lil' Kim attire. There was a woman with goggles on her head who was giving leader vibes. She was pretty, but kept a mean mug and had an aura of power. She pointed toward the VIP section, and immediately they all scattered and walked in different directions. The crowd of over 800 never noticed their militant movements, but if they had, they would have seen that the women were setting up a surveillance perimeter around Natasha. They were just waiting for the green light to kill her.

Courtney was at the Royal Palace eating dinner with Jah'me and Kandy when the conversation turned to Natasha stealing her money. Kandy went on and on about sending her hit squad, but Jah'me quickly intervened and said he would give Courtney the money himself to keep her out of any more trouble. What he didn't know was that Kandy's hit squad had already landed twenty-four hours ago. Even Courtney was unaware. Kandy was just being Kandy and waiting on her little sister to give her the green light. Natasha's ass could be dead within the next hour, but for some reason, Courtney didn't give the word. So, Kandy simply instructed her hitters to follow Natasha's every move until further notice.

For Courtney, it wasn't about the money. It was the cold disrespect and arrogance. She pictured herself beating Natasha's face in and pulling out her hair.

Kandy walked over laughing and said, "No one-on-ones happening, sis. You already know her ass gettin' jumped."

Jah'me sat back laughing at their old asses talking about jumping somebody. He knew they had it in them but could never picture it happening. They were both powerful divas and venting over the dinner table. Before excusing himself, Jah'me offered Courtney the money again. She smiled and respectfully declined. She told him she had unfinished business to handle and wouldn't take his money without honoring her word. Jah'me kissed her on the forehead and wished her luck before leaving the dining hall.

Courtney wasn't broke by a long shot. In fact, she was damn near a billionaire. So, why would she ever take money from her big brother? He was always her ace in the hole when it came to real money. Jah'me was kind-hearted and a cheerful giver, especially when it came to who he considered "his family."

The winners of the Best Dressed contest were a young woman wearing biking shorts, a gold chain, a yellow, red, and black Salt-N-Pepa jacket, and a pair of red 54-11 Reeboks. The male winner rocked a classic red and black Troop sweatsuit, a Kangol bucket hat, a pair of Gazelle designer frames, and fresh suede Bally sneakers. Rumor had it, the giveaway was fake, but when Natasha hit the stage, she made her name known.

"Thank you all for attending my Forever 21 event! Thank you to everyone who participated in the contest. I loved seeing your amazing outfits, but I only have two vehicles to give away tonight. The first Lamborghini, worth two hundred and fifty thousand dollars, goes to Adrian..." She paused while the crowd roared. "The second Lamborghini truck goes to... Rick!"

Natasha passed them both a set of car keys, as they both stood in shock, along with a stunned crowd.

New Jersey Homicide Task Force units arrived on the scene and found Ryan Reynolds dead on arrival. The reporting officer said that Ryan had left a video on his phone just before he shot himself. He showed the video to the two detectives, and they began watching.

Ryan Reynolds appeared to be sweating, distraught, and his eyes were bloodshot red. He stood, holding a .38 Special against his temple. Suddenly, he began talking: "I just walked into my mother's house and saw my entire family murdered in cold blood. This message is for the same person who manipulated, intimidated, and coerced me into testifying in United States Federal Court against Judge Courtney Jones and Aaliyah Huffman, Attorney at Law. I admit, I was scared for my life and my family's. So, I lied on the stand, and she still killed my family!" He began sobbing hysterically.

"When I refused to continue doing her dirty work, this was the result. Well, I'm letting it all out now and that's the honest truth. You can find hundreds of Red Scorpions, kilos of cocaine, and guns at her penthouse and storage units. She had me picking up and dropping off three times a day. I leave you with this information hoping it will free those wrongly accused and bring justice to the accused, cold, cold-hearted killer and mass manipulator, Natasha Bryant."

He cocked the hammer.
BOOM!

Four Weeks Earlier...

Courtney and two of her colleagues arrived at Ryan Reynolds' ranch estate.

The nerve of this fool, she thought. *Ryan hasn't moved yet?*

Upon arriving, she noticed his wife and their four daughters having a picnic in the front yard. "Hello, Sara!"

"Hi, Courtney! How have you been?" Sara asked.

"I'm doing well," Courtney replied.

"My husband hasn't been home in a couple of days. I think the job's been a little strenuous on him lately," she added.

Courtney could tell Sara had no clue what her husband had actually done or the danger she could possibly be in.

Courtney agreed, "Yeah... sometimes, it gets to us. Do you have his new phone number? I have a new case I need his advice on."

"Of course! I have it in my iPhone," Sara said.

"Can you just call him from your phone? I left mine in the car," Courtney replied, knowing full well Ryan wouldn't answer if it came from her number.

Sara passed over her phone and happily returned to her picnic with the girls.

Ryan answered immediately. "Hello, baby!" he said.

"Hello, snitch," Courtney replied coldly. "Now, listen to me, and listen good. You made an oath and broke it, bitch! I've done nothing but right by you, and you got on the stand against me."

"They said it was either immunity or thirty-five to fifty years, Courtney. They were talking about taking my life," he yelled.

"And what the hell you think I'm gonna do?!" she yelled, turning the phone toward his children so he could see them clearly.

"Please," he begged, "not my babies. You can kill me, but please, not my girls."

"I'll spare your family, but under one condition...you kill yourself and make your wrongs right. In the life, we chose and we make sacrifices to get what we want. I need you to help me put Natasha under the jail and I promise you that your daughters will never wipe their own asses. I'll make sure they know you left them well-off. Or we can finish them off right now," Courtney added, flatly.

"No! Not my babies," he cried. "I'll do it."

"Okay, and Ryan...just so you know...I'm far from done with my killing spree. Someone in your family will be dead soon. When this is over, just make sure you put that bullet in your head. It was nice knowing you, coward."

Ryan knew his time breathing was short. With all the wrong he had done, his only wish was for his kids to live their best lives. The only way that would happen was in exchange for his.

Back at the station, detectives received video footage and a phone number from an anonymous source. The video showed Natasha Bryant giving away two Lamborghini trucks at her birthday bash during a Best Dressed contest. Then, they pulled up her social media. She was shopping at Gucci and Prada, flying private to London, and flaunting an extravagant lifestyle. In one post, she stood in a trench mink, dripping in diamonds, beside two Maybach CL650s. The caption read:

If you can't afford two, then you can't afford one.

When the detectives pulled up her tax filings from last year, her earnings didn't come close to supporting the lifestyle she was flaunting. Her reported 2024 income didn't align with her assets. What Natasha didn't realize was that Courtney hadn't reported Natasha's actual salary of $175,000, nor the $50 million signing bonus. She'd even signed the penthouse lease over to Natasha and claimed it had been purchased for $3 million from an anonymous seller.

Just reviewing Natasha's finances led detectives to open a full investigation. Within twenty-four hours, a judge signed a no-knock search warrant.

Meanwhile, in Cape Town, South Africa

Courtney was the real puppet master because she was orchestrating the entire play. She had an extra set of keys to the penthouse. She told Ryan exactly where to place the guns, drugs, and money. Courtney had held back Kandy's hitters for a reason because she needed evidence, not a body. Instead of killing Natasha, they took photos. Surprisingly, Natasha was open and careless enough to let them.

At 5 am, federal agents raided her penthouse and storage units. They confiscated 100 kilos of cocaine, 50 stolen assault weapons, and over $120,000 in petty cash, mostly in tens, twenties, and ones. Natasha was taken out in handcuffs, facing an arsenal of federal charges. After spending a full week in Jersey Central lockup, she finally demanded to have a lawyer present before making any statements.

She waited in the bullpen and tried to piece together what the hell was going on. Natasha was completely oblivious to the charges against her. She had never committed a crime in her life. Yet, here she was, sitting in a jail cell. *Some stuff you just can't make up,* she thought while shaking her head. She had already demanded that a lawyer be present.

About an hour later, a tall, six-foot, bailiff walked up and called her name. Natasha stood to her feet and walked toward him.

"You've got a lawyer visit," he told her, glancing at the paper in his hand.

For the first time since her incarceration, Natasha felt ecstatic. If she could just get a decent attorney, someone who could help her fight back, she knew she had a chance. She clutched her notebook filled with questions she wanted her lawyer to ask the D.A., detectives, and arresting officers.

The questions included:

> **Were any of her fingerprints or DNA on the drugs, guns, or money?**
> **Who were the drugs being distributed to?**
> **Were there any co-defendants or snitches prepared to testify?**

To Natasha, it was a clear setup. To any jury or judge with sense, this case wouldn't hold. She just had to make it to court, and she believed she'd be found not guilty based on circumstantial evidence alone. She sat handcuffed to a steel table. After a long, grueling 45-minute wait, she dozed off from mental exhaustion. That was until the heavy metal door groaned open and someone she never thought she'd see again walked in.

Courtney was on her sister's private Learjet headed back to JFK International. She had just received an email from New Jersey District Attorney Sidney Gardner, stating that her indictments against the United States government had a 90% chance of being dropped. He also requested that she appear at the U.S. District Attorney's office that Monday morning. She replied she'd be there bright and early with her legal team. Three days earlier, Aaliyah had received that information through a trusted source, so she already knew. As soon as she delivered the news, Courtney sent her back stateside to retrieve the money from Natasha.

Now, Natasha sat across the table staring into the face of the woman she thought she'd be testifying against. Aaliyah calmly sat down and opened her briefcase. "Well, hello there," she said with a smirk. "Ain't no fun when the rabbit got the gun, huh?"

"Your license is suspended. You shouldn't even be here!" Natasha snapped.

"That's where you're wrong," Aaliyah said smoothly. "Believe it or not, all our charges have been expunged. We can talk about my beautiful trip to Africa while you were scrambling to gather dirt on me and Courtney, or we can talk deal. I might be able to get you out of here in five years."

"I'd rather die than team up with your criminal ass!" Natasha spat. "You all set me up the same way you set up Anthony!"

"That sounds really dramatic, but the real question is... can you prove it?" Aaliyah raised an eyebrow. "The D.A.'s office has solid evidence on you. You out here living like Bob Barker with your Price Is Right stunts...monthly shopping trips, international vacations, and exotic car giveaways at your 65th birthday party? Girl, really?"

She leaned forward. "The Feds found twenty kilos of fentanyl-based cocaine in your closet, an arsenal of stolen weapons, and over $100K in cash. These are federal charges, Natasha. First offense or not, they'll give you 6 to 25 years in Club Fed." Aaliyah leaned back in her chair. "But I'm your only hope. Why would I help you? Because I know you're innocent and not even my worst enemy deserves what's happening to you." She winked.

"What's the catch?" Natasha asked, cautiously. "And how much is your retainer?"

Aaliyah started swaying in her seat and humming as if she were dancing to a reggae tune only she could hear. Natasha could tell she was enjoying herself way too much.

After a brief pause, Aaliyah pulled out her phone. "Let me text my superior," she said. A moment later, she looked back up. "Okay, we came up with a light estimate."

"How much?"

Aaliyah leaned in, serious now. "Three hundred million dollars."

Natasha froze.

"We both know you took Courtney's money. Just give it back...with interest. That's the deal. Take it or leave it."

Natasha sat in silence. She knew Aaliyah was just a messenger. A pawn. Courtney was the real puppet master. She was pulling all of the strings, making the calls, and manipulating every negotiation. If this plea deal could actually get her out...if there was a chance she could avoid life in prison...then maybe, just maybe, she'd consider it.

Meanwhile, at Leavenworth Federal Correctional Facility in Kentucky, Courtney stayed inside her luxury Cadillac truck. She didn't need to go in because she had people for that. An hour later, Anthony Brown was escorted into the visitation room, shackled and handcuffed.

"What is this about?" he asked, confused.

A sharply dressed man in a tailored Tom Ford suit stood to greet him. A Rolex peeked from under his cuff as he extended his hand. "Danny Smith," the man said. "High-powered attorney. Courtney's business partner."

At the mention of Courtney's name, Anthony shook his head in disgust.

Danny smirked because he understood exactly what this meant. He opened his briefcase and slid a document across the table. "She sent a proposition," he said, his tone flat but firm. "Her words...not mine...it's non-negotiable. She wants you to testify against Natasha Bryant before the grand jury. In return, she'll personally make sure you're granted immunity and released after Natasha is convicted."

Anthony sat silently for a moment and thought it through. Danny continued, "She's also offering a token of appreciation. A total of three hundred million dollars...for your cooperation."

Anthony's eyes widened, and his energy shifted.

"She better not jerk me with the money!" he snapped.

Danny chuckled. "You know her just as well as I do. She pays like she weighs. Her word is always solid."

Anthony nodded slowly. "Give me the damn papers."

He signed every last one.

Two Weeks Later...

Anthony arrived at the Federal Courthouse, shackled and dressed in an orange jumpsuit. The courtroom buzzed with attorneys, reporters, and jurors. This was a high-profile case of corruption, and the tension in the air was thick. Once the jurors took their seats, Anthony was brought in and escorted to the witness stand.

A petite white woman stepped up, holding a Bible. "Mr. Brown," she said. "Do you swear to tell the truth, the whole truth, and nothing but the truth, so help you God?"

"I do," Anthony replied.

"You may proceed, Counselor," the judge said, nodding to the District Attorney.

"Mr. Brown, for the record, have you been promised anything or forced to testify today?"

"No," Anthony said.

"You are currently incarcerated in a federal corrections facility in Kentucky?"

"Yes."

"And you're testifying with the assumption that your cooperation might lead to a sentence reduction?"

"Yes."

Anthony was starting to sweat under the courtroom lights. It felt like everything was being laid bare. So, he figured he might as well make it convincing.

"Natasha Rene Bryant...who is she to you?"

"She's the person I distributed kilos of cocaine for," he answered plainly.

"And for the record, can you point to a photo of Ms. Bryant for the jury?"

Anthony glanced at a lineup of twelve women. Natasha's mugshot looked more like a glamour shot than anything else. He picked her out instantly. The jurors looked stunned.

"Let the record show that Mr. Brown identified the accused, Natasha Bryant."

"How long has this operation been going on?" the prosecutor asked.

"I'd say I did business with Ms. Bryant for over five years."

The prosecutor turned to the jury. "Let the record also state that Ms. Natasha Bryant operated a law firm during those years. This type of corruption spits in the face of our justice system and everything we stand for under the banner of freedom and liberty." She turned to the judge. "I ask that the court take Mr. Brown's testimony into consideration and proceed accordingly."

The judge nodded. The indictments were sealed. The jury was dismissed. Anthony was escorted back to the bullpen. Kandy sat quietly at the back of the courtroom and watched everything. She and Anthony exchanged brief eye contact. He knew exactly who she was. Kandy exited the courtroom and slid into the back seat of a luxury Rolls-Royce where her sister waited.

"It went well," Kandy said. "The judge accepted his testimony. Now, we're just waiting on the call from the District Attorney, right?"

"Yes, girl," Courtney replied, a satisfied smile on her face. "That should come within a few hours. Once all the indictments are sealed."

Back at the jail, Natasha had no clue Anthony had just testified before a federal grand jury. In fact, she didn't even know who he was. Courtney's orchestration was pure genius. Simply, a masterclass in manipulation. She had been targeting Natasha from the beginning, ever since she stumbled across her social media. Natasha, the flashy attorney who flaunted a lifestyle she could barely afford.

Courtney saw through it instantly.

Natasha was drowning in debt, behind on rent for her tiny New York office, leasing a Maybach she could barely afford, and faking a high life on Instagram. Courtney saw an opportunity and pounced. It was never personal. Natasha wasn't the enemy. She was just collateral damage. The sacrificial lamb in Courtney's rise to power.

Eventually, Natasha arranged to have the money wired to an anonymous bank account. A few days later, she received a letter from Aaliyah confirming receipt of payment. She sat back, stared at the ceiling of her cell, and wondered how she could have ever thought she could get away with stealing that kind of money without consequences.

Her cellmate Kim interrupted her thoughts. "You want this bologna sandwich?"

"You can have it every time," Natasha muttered. "I'll starve first."

The indictment of Natasha Bryant made national headlines. On the courthouse steps, Judge Courtney Jones stood beside Prosecuting Attorney Steve Savage, addressing a crowd of over a thousand and dozens of news cameras.

"I stood strong in the midst of flames," Courtney declared. "I forged through the fire knowing I would come out refined. I bleed integrity, honesty, loyalty, and justice for all. Thank you to each and every person who had my back through these trying days. Justice has prevailed! To the people of New

Jersey, I ask that you continue to believe in our justice system because it works."

Steve Savage stepped up next. He thanked the people for their support before both of them waved and exited the stage.

Back at the jail, Natasha watched the broadcast from her cell, shaking her head. She knew Courtney was a master manipulator...a criminal-minded strategist...but she couldn't prove it.

Not yet.

Christmas Eve, 8:00 AM – Leavenworth Federal Penitentiary

Anthony Brown stepped out of the prison gates with nothing but the clothes on his back, a bus ticket, and a thousand dollars in cash. The cold air hit him like a slap, but the freedom warmed him inside. He climbed into the waiting corrections van and headed for the bus station. He was relieved to be out, but guilt weighed heavily on his shoulders. Testifying against Natasha went against everything he believed in. The streets had a code, and he broke it.

No excuses.

No justifications.

Regardless of how dirty things had gotten, he'd crossed a line. The game wasn't for him anymore. He planned to head south, stay low, and restart his life working at a warehouse or driving a Sprinter van. His grandmother's home in South Carolina felt like the right place to reset.

That plan dissolved the moment he looked up and spotted a burgundy Rolls-Royce Wraith Coupe with dark tints and 32" rims pulling in. The driver stepped out.

It was Aaliyah.

She wore a tiny miniskirt that showed off her long, shapely legs that shimmered in the sunlight. Her stiletto heels clicked against the pavement, and her silky hair flowed down to the small of her back.

"My God, Aaliyah," Anthony said as his eyes devoured her. "You look good enough to eat."

She laughed. "Come with me."

He obeyed without hesitation.

Thirty Minutes Later – Private Airstrip

The Wraith pulled into a hangar, where Courtney waited at the foot of a gleaming Learjet. Anthony boarded the jet, only to be greeted by familiar faces: Steve Savage, Danny Smith, Michelle... and of course, Aaliyah.

"Welcome home, Ace," Courtney said with a sly smile.

He smirked, though the fire in his eyes hadn't cooled. "If that's what you want to call it. I stayed in prison for almost a year, Courtney... behind something you set in motion."

She let him vent. She knew he needed to.

After twenty minutes, she spoke. "You're right. I was wrong for leaving you in there that long, but I never meant for you to stay down. Sometimes, someone's got to take one for the team to get us to the top, and you did that. For that, we thank you."

She stood, her voice steady and commanding. "This family's been tested beyond measure, and we're still standing. I want to offer you a key position in The Firm as my lieutenant. Your offshore account has been activated with the three hundred million you were promised. I added a bonus to cover your investments and losses."

She extended her hand. "To the Firm."

Anthony looked around the room. Every pair of eyes was on him and glasses of champagne were raised in a silent toast. He reached out and shook her hand.

"To the Firm."

The room erupted in celebration.

Meanwhile, Natasha Bryant was sentenced to five years in a federal correctional facility in West Virginia. Three years into her sentence, she received an unexpected deposit—over $100,000. The money kept coming. It was $20,000 here, $30,000 there, and it was every couple of months. She had no idea who was sending it.

On New Year's Eve, year three of her sentence, Natasha sat across from Aaliyah in the visitation room. Her face was fuller and her body was thicker because prison had changed her appearance.

"Well damn," Aaliyah grinned, "somebody's been eating like a fat cat."

Natasha laughed. "Yeah, I always wanted a big butt, but not like this."

"You're wearing it well. What size are you now?"

"Went from a three to a five."

"Well, I was sent with a message," Aaliyah said, her tone shifting.

"I figured," Natasha nodded.

"Courtney said every member of the family takes one for the team. That's what makes us a family...unity and loyalty. You started the drama, but she still respects you as a businesswoman. She's the one who's been sending you the money."

Natasha's eyes widened. "Our Firm is a family. Courtney is the commander-in-chief. She wants to offer you something big. She wants to offer you a chance to live the life you always dreamed of."

"I'm listening."

"We need someone to run the West Coast operations such as the law offices, bail bonds, and... distribution. You'd oversee it all."

Natasha leaned in. "I can do that."

"Good. Trust, you'll be compensated well. Keep your head up."

Aaliyah stood and walked away.

Mission accomplished.

Back in New Jersey

Courtney updated the team. The Firm was expanding its empire west. Law offices. Bail bonds. Drugs. Investments were maturing, and joint venture payouts had landed.

She wired each member $15 million.

"The hustle doesn't stop," she told her inner circle, toasting yet another windfall.

January 1st – Natasha's Release

At 9 am sharp, Natasha walked out of the prison gates after serving 54 months. Michelle greeted her at the curb and ushered her into a black Mercedes. By 10 am, they arrived at the airport. Michelle handed her a flight itinerary and instructions.

When Natasha landed in California, a driver met her and led her to a sprawling estate that took her breath away. It looked like a $10 million property. There were brand new foreign cars lined the driveway with stickers still on the windows.

Three tall, armed Spanish men stepped forward. "Your security," one said. "Twenty-four-seven."

She was introduced to her maids and butlers. Everything she needed was at her beck and call. Her master bedroom made her jaw drop. Every luxury designer label filled her walk-in closet, all in size five. The jewelry boxes within her closet sparkled with over a million dollars in watches, necklaces, and bracelets.

That was when it hit her.

This wasn't just a family.

Courtney's firm was a billion-dollar cartel, and Natasha had just committed her life to it.

You just read another Uptown Classic. Please be on the lookout for Part 2 of this epic, Courtney Jones' four-book series. Shout out to my hardworking publisher, CiCi Merie, at Merie Vision Publishing. We got another one. I also want to give thanks to everyone who has read my books and has been supporting me throughout this amazing journey.

A special thanks to my day one fans for believing in me when no one knew who Jeremy Jae-Jae Davis was. I told you all back then that I wasn't going to stop. The industry is in trouble the very moment I get my foot in the door. Until then, I'm going to continue to give you my best creativity to the best of my ability. Thank you once again.

Uptown Classic and Merie Vision's – we're taking over the industry one book at a time!

Made in the USA
Columbia, SC
14 July 2025